Mary Cowden Clarke

**Uncle, Peep, And I**

A Child's Novel

Mary Cowden Clarke

**Uncle, Peep, And I**
*A Child's Novel*

ISBN/EAN: 9783743435551

Printed in Europe, USA, Canada, Australia, Japan

Cover: Foto ©Andreas Hilbeck / pixelio.de

More available books at **www.hansebooks.com**

"I found myself staring up at a strange man's face that was staring down at us." — PAGE 13.

# A Child's Novel.

BY

## MARY COWDEN-CLARKE,

AUTHOR OF

THE "COMPLETE CONCORDANCE TO SHAKESPEARE," THE "SHAKESPEARE KEY,"
"GIRLHOOD OF SHAKESPEARE'S HEROINES," "KIT BAM'S ADVENTURES,"
"MANY HAPPY RETURNS OF THE DAY," THE "IRON COUSIN,"
"A RAMBLING STORY," ETC., ETC.

Let us from point to point this story know,
To make the even truth in pleasure flow.

SHAKESPEARE.

BOSTON:
ROBERTS BROTHERS.
1886.

University Press:
JOHN WILSON AND SON, CAMBRIDGE.

TO

# MY MANY DEAR KIND FRIENDS

## *IN AMERICA,*

AND

# TO THEIR CHILDREN,

𝕿𝖍𝖎𝖘 𝕭𝖔𝖔𝖐 𝖎𝖘 𝕯𝖊𝖉𝖎𝖈𝖆𝖙𝖊𝖉,

WITH AFFECTIONATE ESTEEM AND GRATITUDE.

# PREFACE.

URING a summer ramble in Germany, while making some stay at delightful Dresden, I met a sweet-faced American lady, who looked scarcely older than her two fair young daughters, so fresh was her complexion, and who said to me, "I wish you would write something for our American children which would make them know and love you as we all have long known and loved you through your pen."

On my return to my Italian home, I thought over her obliging words; and one morning I awoke with the sketch presented to my mind of " Uncle, Peep, and I," which I thought afforded scope for fulfilment of her wish. The style of "Dutch painting," which I adopted for this child's novel, is in accordance with what I remember wishing for in my childhood days, when I liked to know every detail of a narrative, and asked, " Well, what did *he* say? "   " Then, what did *she* say? "   The incidents are chosen that may best develop the questions of graciousness or ungraciousness in manner, kindliness or unaffectionateness in gift and acceptance, the enjoyment that lies in simple and inexpensive pleasures, — questions that are often unconsciously yet keenly felt by sensitive and naturally tasteful children ; while the English figures, English landscape, English park scenery, in my picture have been delineated as likely to attract and interest my young American readers, and incline them to take into their favor

Their friend and well-wisher,

MARY COWDEN-CLARKE.

VILLA NOVELLO, GENOA.
  *February*, 1886.

# UNCLE, PEEP, AND I.

## CHAPTER I.

USH! Don't cry so, Peep."

"You're crying yourself, Bab."

"I'm trying not to cry, Peep."

"So am I, Bab; but I can't help crying. When I saw those men come and take father away, I cried; and I've been crying ever since. Where did they take him to, Bab?"

"To heaven, Peep."

"Where's that, Bab? Is it far?"

"Oh, ever so far, Peep; it must be."

"But where is it, Bab?"

"I don't know, Peep."

Peep stopped a minute to think; then he said, —

"Why do you think it's far off, Bab?"

"Because when mother died, Peep, father told me she was gone to heaven; and she never came back, so I thought it must be a long way off. And now he's gone, too, — to look after her, I suppose; and very likely he will never come back either."

Peep and I began to cry afresh then, and went on crying. But presently he looked at me again, and said, —

"Do people always go to heaven in a long box, Bab?"

"What do you mean, Peep?"

"I mean I saw those men put father in a great long box when they took him away; and that was what made me cry most of all, Bab; it looked so odd and so — "

Peep broke off, partly as if he did n't know what word to use, partly as if crying stopped his speaking.

"Don't sob so, Peep; try and think of father before he grew ill, and when he used to talk and laugh and play with us, to keep us from feeling dull and too hungry, when he had little to bring home for us to eat."

"I'm hungry now, Bab."

"Are you, Peep? I'm afraid there's not much in the cupboard. But I'll look."

I found a piece of bread, which I had put away when I couldn't eat at breakfast-time, while the men came to carry father away. So I gave it to Peep, who began to munch it slowly; for it was very hard, and he could hardly get his teeth into it. He was only five years old, poor little fellow, and I wasn't much older, though I seemed so; for father used to tell me things about mother, and how she would have taught me to be like a little mother to Peep if she hadn't had to go away to heaven so soon; and I tried to be like one as well as I could by what he told me of her. I was thinking about all this when Peep said, —

"Ain't *you* hungry, too, Bab?"

"Not very, Peep; not so hungry as you are."

"How do you know, Bab?"

"Oh, I'm sure of it, Peep; I see you're hungry, — *very* hungry, and I'm only *rather* hungry."

"I'm very cold, too, Bab, and there's no fire in the grate."

"No, Peep, and I can't light one, for there's no wood left, and very little coal." .

"What shall we do, Bab?"

"Let's sit down together on the rug, Peep, and wrap ourselves up in it; it'll keep us warm."

Peep's teeth were chattering, and he trembled a good deal when we first sat down on the rug; but after we had hunched ourselves close together and wrapped it round us both, we felt rather better, and he said, —

"What a cross old thing that Mrs. Wall is, isn't she, Bab?"

"Yes, she's very cross, Peep; but she brought us some milk for breakfast this morning, and I don't think she could have been paid for it; for father said last night he hadn't a shilling left, and how we should get any breakfast he didn't know; so it must have been some milk she gave us for kindness, though she *is* cross, Peep."

Peep said nothing for some time, and at last I felt him lean heavily against me ; so heavily and so lumpily that I knew he must be asleep, and I kept myself from moving for fear of waking him. I suppose I must have fallen asleep too, for I don't remember anything else till I found myself staring up from the folds of the rug at a strange man's face, that was staring down at us as we lay there wrapped up together.

" What are you at ? " said the strange man, in a gruffish voice.

" We're trying to keep ourselves warm," I said.

" What's your names ? "

" Peep and Bab," I answered.

" All right ; you're the little 'uns I came to look after. Your mother told me of you in the last letter she wrote to me out there, and asked me, when I returned, to come and see after you. I'm returned, — from sea, — and am come. She's gone, I suppose. I knew, from her letter, she could n't last long, poor soul. Poor girl ! Poor Dolly ! "

The man put up his arm and brushed his coat-sleeve over his eyes.

"Father used to call her Dolly, too; but her real name was Dorothy," I ventured to whisper.

"Ay, ay; all right. You're my poor sister's little 'uns, sure enough. Where's your father?"

"Gone, too. They carried him away to heaven this very morning. If mother was your sister, you must be Uncle that she used to tell us of," I added, staring still harder up in his face.

"Yes, I'm Uncle; your uncle; Uncle John Bruff. Come along with me, young 'uns; you can't stay here, you know, all by yourselves. Come, come along with me."

So saying, Uncle gave me a strong tug, and gave Peep another, which pulled us up on to our feet. Peep had been rubbing his eyes, and waking, and staring up, too, at the strange man with the gruffish voice. Just then Mrs. Wall came into the room, and Uncle went to her and spoke some words

with her, and gave her some money; and
then he turned to us again, took one of us
in each hand, and walked quickly downstairs
to the street-door, where there was a hackney-
coach waiting, into which he lifted Peep and
me. As we drove along, Uncle did n't look
much at us, but kept staring out of the coach
window, and seemed to be thinking hard and
not noticing what he saw in the streets. We
went through a good many, and at last came
to roads and lanes with trees and hedges
on each side. Peep crept closer still to me,
— he had kept close to me all the time, —
and, as he peered out on our side of the
coach, he whispered to me, —

"Oh, Bab, we 're in the country!"

"Yes, Peep, in the real country. How
nice and green it is!"

"Do you think he 's going to steal us?"
said Peep, with a frightened glance at
Uncle.

"No, Peep, I don't think so; we ain't
worth stealing, and though his voice is gruff,
he don't seem really cross. He is n't going

to do anything bad to us, I think.  He called
mother ' poor girl,' you know."

" Did he, Bab?"

" Yes, and ' poor Dolly.'  I think he 's
going to be good to us, for her sake."

" If he 's going to be good, why does he
talk like being angry, Bab?"

"I don't know, Peep.  Some people do
talk rough though they mean to be kind.
Mrs. Wall did."

" So she did," said Peep, nodding his
head and falling silent again.  Presently he
whispered, —

" Oh, I *am* so hungry, Bab."

But just as he said this he nearly tumbled
off his seat; for the coach stopped with a
sudden jerk, and we found ourselves before
the garden-gate of a house among trees;
though by this time the evening was coming
on, and I could n't see much of the place we
were being taken to.

Uncle lifted us out as he had lifted us in,
and then took us, one in each hand, along
a little path that led to the door of the house,

calling out as he did so, in a loud, roaring voice, —

"Ahoy! Sal! Where are you? Sal! Sal!"

A light came to the door; it opened, and a servant-girl appeared.

"Take these young 'uns into the parlor, Sal, while I go and give coachee his fare."

Sal stared at us, repeating, "Young 'uns!" then took us from Uncle's hands, and turned with us into a room where I was almost blinded by the bright light of a blazing fire and of two candles on the table, on which there was a white table-cloth, and plates, and knives and forks shining and glittering in the candlelight.

Sal muttered something grumpily to herself that I could n't make out; but when Uncle came in, she turned to him, and said in a snappish tone, —

"You did n't say nothing about bringing child'n home with you. But supper for one 's supper for two, or for three, for that matter; so I s'pose there 's enough, Cap'n."

"Yes, yes, of course there 's enough; so

bring in supper, sharp, Sal,— sharp, d' ye hear ; for I 'll bet these young 'uns are sharp-set."

" That I 'll be bound ! " said Sal, as she bounced out, and soon bounced in again, bringing hot meat, and potatoes, and bread, with which Uncle heaped our plates and his own.    Then Sal brought in a tray with glasses, and a jug of hot·water, and a bottle with a bright ticket hung round its neck, from which Uncle poured some strong-smelling stuff into three glasses, filling them up with hot water.

" Have some grog, Bab and Peep; it 'll do you good, and put some warmth into you after your long, cold drive."

Peep and I took what Uncle called " grog ; " but it was so boiling hot and so strong that it nearly took away our breath as we tried to sip some.   Uncle watched us, and laughed a loud laugh at the way in which we drew our lips suddenly back; but when he put another lump of sugar into our glasses and the " grog " was a little cooler, Peep gulped

it down, and soon after fell fast asleep and
nearly toppled off his chair.          •

"Sal, take the young shaver to bed," said
Uncle, still laughing.

"Let me go with him," I said.   "I always
put Peep to bed, and he won't be comfortable
if I don't."

"Ay, ay, all right ; off with you too, Bab ;
a couple of rum young 'uns you are, and no
mistake.   But I must make the best of you
I can, I s'pose, for poor Dolly's sake, poor
girl ! "

Sal lifted Peep up in her strong, red arms,
and I followed her upstairs.   She led the way
into a small room, with a white-curtained
window and a white-curtained bed, muttering
sulkily, —

"Men are all alike !   No thought for anything !   It's a mercy Master Tom's away
at school, or there'd ha' been no bed for
these child'n.   But they can lie in his for
to-night, and to-morrow I'll make 'em up
one in t' other room."

As soon as Sal had put Peep down on

an arm-chair there was by the bedside, she
bounced out, and returned with a couple of
nightgowns, saying, —

" There ! you can have Master Tom's night-
clothes till he comes back, and by then I
s'pose the Cap'n 'll have had some made for
you both your own selves."

I thanked her, and soon had Peep undressed
and snugly tucked up in bed, while Sal stood
by and looked at me. Suddenly she burst
out with, —

" Well, I never ! That bit of a gal might
be an old .'oman, for the gumptionable way
she fettles up her little brother ! "

I was n't long in getting undressed myself ;
and then, after giving Peep a hearty kiss as
his white, tired-out face lay on the pillow,
comfortably resting there, I laid myself down
beside him and waited till Sal went out of
the room. Then I softly got up and knelt
down near the bed, as mother taught me, and
asked God to pity and help us ; and then I
slipped into bed again, and was soon fast
asleep.

## CHAPTER II.

NEXT morning I awoke long before Peep, and crept out o' bed quietly that I might n't wake him. I went to the window and lifted up the white curtain that hung before it and looked out. I nearly cried out when I saw what was there, it was all so pretty and so pleasant. There were the trees and grass-plot and path-way I had half made out overnight, and there was a bright blue sky above them, in which some white pigeons were flying round and round, and there was a little bird singing on a bush quite close to the house. I could see him quite plainly, perching there, and could hear his loud chirping voice as clearly as possible. I stood there a good while, listen-ing and looking, and found myself thanking God for sending me to a place where I could

see and hear all this, before I remembered
to kneel down and thank him in the words
mother taught me. Then I thought I would
get ready dressed and washed before Peep
awoke and wanted me to dress and wash
him.

"Where are we, Bab?" were his first
words as he started up, leaning on his elbow
and staring round the room.

"We're where Uncle brought us, Peep,
yesterday; don't you recollect? The coach,
the coming into the country, the stopping at
a house with a garden, the supper, the hot
'grog,' as Uncle called it, — don't you remember it all?"

"Yes, I think I do, Bab; but what place
do you fancy it is?"

"I s'pose it's his home, Peep."

"Do you think he means us to live in it, —
to live with him, Bab?"

"Well, I don't know; I suppose he does,
Peep. How should you like to live here with
him?"

"Oh, I don't mind; I shouldn't care to stay

here with him by myself, Bab; but if he's going to have you and me both to stay with him, I would n't mind. That was a good supper last night, — I *was* so hungry, Bab, — though I don't like the ' grog ; ' it was so burning, — not only hot, you know, but so stinging, somehow; it hurt my throat when I tried to swallow it for fear he should be angry if I did n't, when he had told me to drink it up."

"I hope he won't bid us to drink any more ' grog,' Peep, and then all the rest I like. Not only the supper was good, — *I* was hungry, too, oh, *so* hungry, Peep! — but it was good to have a bed to sleep upon, and night-clothes to put on, and, oh, Peep! *such* a nice garden to look out at! Do come and see what there is at this window, — pigeons, trees, grass, — oh, so green, so very, very pretty ! "

Peep scrambled out of bed in a hurry; and when he and I had looked out till he began to shiver a little, and I recollected it was too cold for him to be staying there without his clothes, I began to wash and dress him quickly; so that when Sal came bouncing in, she found us both ready.

"Well, I never!" she exclaimed; "that gal beats all I ever see in the way of old 'omanish gumption! She has more nouse than many a married 'oman I know, in regard to being a mother to her little brother there. Come, both on you; as you're ready dressed a'ready, you can come down and be in the parlor for breakfast before the Cap'n himself is down."

However, this was not the case; for we found Uncle standing with his back to the fire, his coat-tails under his arms and a newspaper in his hand, as we went into the room where breakfast was spread on the table and looked very nice, it was so plentiful and good. There was a pile of thick bread and butter on a plate, and on another were some slices of fried ham and eggs, while hooked on to the fender was still another plate, with a tall heap of buttered toast upon it, to keep hot before the fire. A coffee-pot, a milk-jug, and a sugar-basin stood on the table, with an uncut crusty loaf and a large pat of butter.

I saw Peep cast a longing look at all these good things; but I nudged him, and whispered, —

"Come and say good morning to Uncle, Peep."

We took hold of hands and walked straight up to the rug where Uncle stood behind the big newspaper, which nearly hid him from us, and said, —

"Good morning, Uncle."

He nodded, without taking his eyes off the newspaper; then, putting one of his fingers on the line he had been reading, he lowered the large sheet and looked over its top at us two.

"'Morning, Bab and Peep. Stop a bit; wait till I've finished this bit about the 'Shipping Intelligence;' then sharp's the word for breakfast."

In a few minutes Uncle laid down the big paper, and took his seat at the table, nodding to us to take ours also. He helped himself and us to huge portions of the good things there, and we all three ate on in silence for some time, till suddenly Peep leaned towards me and whispered, —

" Bab! Look at that cow on the butter! Ain't it well done? But what do they put a cow on the butter for?"

I looked at the pat of butter and saw there was a cow, as Peep said, upon it; but I did n't know why it was put there, so I only said, —

" Hush, Peep; don't ask questions now; I 'll tell you about it afterwards."

" What are you two young 'uns whispering about, — hatching mischief, or what?" said Uncle, gruffly.

" Ain't hatching anything, Uncle," I plucked up courage to say.

" Ain't you, though? What are you whispering? Out with it."

" We want to know what a cow 's put on the butter for, Uncle."

Uncle laughed his loud, roaring laugh; then he said, —

" A cow gives milk; milk makes cream;

cream makes butter. That's it; don't you see?"

Peep nodded. "I see," he said.

"Well, I'm off to town. Must go to Lloyd's," said Uncle, starting up from table as he finished breakfast. "Amuse yourselves, young 'uns; run about in the garden as much as you like. By-by.

He went quickly out, walked briskly along the garden-path, and went out of the gate, giving it a sharp bang behind him.

Peep and I slipped off our chairs and ran into the garden, where we played about till we were tired, and went to sit upon a garden-seat under a tree to enjoy the shade. Presently we saw a lad in a smock-frock, with a wheelbarrow full of some dark stuff, come into the garden by a side-gate towards the back of the house. He saw us, and let go the handle on one side of the barrow, that he might lift his hand to his hair and twitch one lock as he looked at us; then he trundled his barrow towards a flower-bed near, and began strewing the dark stuff among the

flowers. We both watched him, till at last
Peep said, —

"Why does that boy put dirt there, Bab?
It looks so nasty, and smells nastier. Why
does he do it?"

"I don't know, Peep."

"It'll dirty the roses. I've a good mind
to tell him not to do it, Bab."

"P'rhaps he's been told to do it, Peep;
he'd hardly do it if Uncle or Sal had n't told
him he might."

"Oh, they could n't have told him to strew
that mess in this nice garden, Bab; I'll ask
him if they did. He don't look like a bad
boy in his face, though he's scattering dirt;
so I'm not afraid of him."

Peep slid off the garden-seat and went
straight up to the lad in the smock-frock,
who left off what he was about to twitch the
lock of hair on his forehead again.

"What are you doing that for? You'll
spoil the roses, putting that dirt among 'em.
Were you told to do it?"

"Oh, mook don't spoil roses; it makes 'em

grow beautiful, it do. Cap'n Brooff has me at odd times to do a bit o' gardening here, and to-day I brought a barrowful o' mook for the rose-bed."

"Mook?" said Peep.

"Yes, little master, mook, — doong, you know, — horse-doong; Cap'n and the gentle-folks sometimes calls it manoor."

This boy had a nubbly, ugly face, but a very nice-looking face, too; at least, I liked it, and did n't wonder Peep had n't felt afraid of speaking to him. I did n't feel afraid of him either, so I said, —

"'Cap'n?' You mean Captain Bruff; Uncle, our Uncle."

"Yes, little miss, Cap'n Brooff. He's come to live here lately, and gives me a job now and then, and lets me do a hand's turn in the garden between-times."

"Between-times?" said Peep.

"Yes, little master; at odd hours, off and on, when I ain't got other work. I mostly get work at farmer Giles's; but when farmer Giles don't want extra hands, Cap'n

takes me on here. I'm mortal fond o'
gardening."

"Are you?" asked Peep.

"Yes, and I'm fond o' gardening *here;* for
Cap'n Brooff's a nice gen'l'man to work for,
though he's a bit rough o' speech, and sounds
harder than he is."

"That's true," I said.

"How do you know, Bab? We've only
seen him since yesterday," said Peep.

"Well, I know it, Peep, because though he
speaks gruff and short he lifted us into the
coach and out of the coach gently, and did n't
hurt me a bit when he snatched me up to do
it; and then he brought us to where we got
a good supper and a good breakfast when
we'd nothing to eat where we were before,
and to a house with this nice garden instead
of a house with houses opposite and nothing
but streets all round to look at."

Peep did n't answer this, but kept steadily
watching the lad strewing the contents of his
barrow among the flowers. At last Peep
leaned towards me, still keeping his eye

fixed on the lad, and whispered in my ear, —

"I wonder what his name is, Bab."

"Ask him, Peep; you ain't afraid of him, you know."

"No, I ain't afraid of him. His face is n't cross, and his voice is n't fierce, is it, Bab?"

"No, Peep, I like his face and his voice too."

"So do I. I say, boy, what's your name?" said Peep, raising his own voice.

The lad looked up, pulled his lock of hair, and said, —

"Ned Carter."

"Should you mind giving me a ride in that barrow, Ned Carter, when you've emptied it all out?" said Peep.

"Not I, little master," said Ned, with his cheery, brisk voice. "It'll soon be empty now, and I'll just give it a rub down clean after the mook's out, so it sha'n't do no hurt to your clothes."

"P'rhaps it'll make 'em smell," I whispered to Peep.

But he was too eager for his ride in the barrow to recollect what he himself had said about the nasty stuff and its nastier smell; so he clambered in, and Ned Carter wheeled him twice round the garden; then he said, —

"Now, little master, you'll have to get out; because Cap'n Brooff pays me to work, not play."

"Do you think it play to wheel me about?" asked Peep, as he let Ned lift him down.

"Why, to be sure it is, little master."

"Well, then, Ned, I should like to have some play with you again, next time you come to work here."

"You'll have to ask Uncle to let him play a little with you, Peep, as well as work in the garden," I said.

"I don't think I shall like to ask Uncle that, or ask him anything, Bab; I'm afraid of *him*, though I ain't of Ned Carter."

"But I ain't afraid, — that is, *much* afraid, of Uncle, Peep, and if you like, *I'll* ask him to let you have some play with Ned some day."

"Oh, that would be nice, Bab! Do, do! Mind you don't forget, for I should like to play with Ned; he looks as if he'd be a good playfellow, and not mind having a game with me though I am so much littler than he is."

We stayed in the garden watching Ned as he went about working among the flowers, till at last he gave a tug to his front hair, said, " Good-day t' ye, little miss and little master," and went away pulling his empty barrow behind him.

We went into the house, where Sal gave Peep and me a hunk of bread and cheese apiece, saying, —

" I s'pose you child'n 'll not be able to last out till Cap'n comes home to dinner; he don't come home till latish, ever, and sometimes he don't come back till supper-time. But he said he'd be home to dinner to-day nigh upon four."

" What's ' Lloyd's,' Sal ? " I asked.

" What in the name o' patience does the child mean?" was Sal's reply.

" Uncle said he was going to ' Lloyd's,'

3

when he went out this morning," I replied.
" He said he was off to town, and must go to
'Lloyd's.' So, what's 'Lloyd's'? I mean,
where's 'Lloyd's'? Is it in town, in London?"

" How should I know what it is or where
it is?" said Sal, snappishly. "But," she
added, sniffing up her nose sharply, "what
on earth have you two plagues o' child'n
been up to? Where have you been?"

" In the garden," I answered.

" The whole time? Not gone outside?
Let me catch you going out o' the gate,
that's all, without leave! Did you stay in
the garden all the while?"

" Yes," we both said at once.

Suddenly Sal caught hold of Peep by the
shoulder, and said, —

" It's you; you've been a-rolling on the
ground where Ned's been manoorin the rose-
bed, and a fine job I shall have to make you
sweet and clean before Cap'n comes home.
It's fit to p'ison him while he dines, it is!"

" Never mind, Sal, *I'll* clean up Peep,"
I said. "Here, Peep, come upstairs with

me, and I'll manage to make you all right by the time Uncle comes back to dinner."

" Well, that bit of a gal's as good as a play, with her old-fashioned motherly ways," I heard her mutter, as she bounced off to the kitchen; and I went up to the room where we had slept last night, and took off Peep's jacket and trousers, and wiped them with a damp towel, and hung them out of window till they lost the bad smell and were quite dry for him to put on again.

By the time this was done, I heard Uncle's loud, roaring voice below, and Peep and I went downstairs to be ready for dinner. He nodded at us when we came into the parlor, and we took our seats at the table, on which the cloth was already laid, and Sal soon served the meat. When she took it away and put some cheese and radishes on the table, Uncle suddenly said, —

" Why didn't you give us a pudd'n', Sal? These young 'uns would have liked something sweet, I'll bet."

" You never give orders for none, Cap'n."

"No, but you might ha' guessed, Sal."

"How should I ha' guessed? How should I ha' known you 'd ha' chose to go to the expense of a pudd'n' besides meat for these child'n, when you don't never have one done for yourself, Cap'n?"

"Oh, *me?* I 'm quite another thing; I ain't got a sweet tooth in my head, but I s'pose these young 'uns have; young 'uns always have."

I thought it so good-natured of Uncle to say this, that I felt able now to get out what I had to ask him, and said, —

"Uncle, please would you mind letting Ned Carter play a little with Peep next time he comes to garden here? It would n't take him *very* long from his work."

Uncle laid down his knife, with a bit of cheese stuck on the tip of it, that he was just going to put into his mouth, and stared hard at me. Then he said, —

"Peep 's rum, but you 're rummer, Bab, — a sight rummer; not a doubt about it."

Then he closed his lips round the bit of

cheese, snapped off a morsel of radish, and pinched off a piece of crust of bread, which he crunched up all together, still keeping his eyes fixed on me.

I saw he wasn't angry, though he stared with such a grave look; so I said, —

"Please, Uncle, would you?"

He nodded.

"To be sure, child; why shouldn't I? It's nat'ral in young 'uns to like play, I s'pose. We grown-ups like play now and then, too, o' course."

He went on slowly finishing his bread and cheese and radishes, never taking his eyes off me, and then he said, —

"That's for Peep; haven't you anything to ask me for yourself, Bab?"

"Yes, Uncle; where's 'Lloyd's'?"

He suddenly dropped his knife with a clang on to his plate, and said, —

"What?"

"Where's 'Lloyd's,' Uncle, — the place you said you were going to this morning, you know? Is it in London? Is it

near where we lived? Is it near Mrs.
Wall's?"

"Of all the rum gals I ever — Well, it's
not so very far from that alley I found you
in ; but what do you want to know for?"

"Because next time you go to 'Lloyd's,'
Uncle, please would you take me with
you?"

"Take you with me to 'Lloyd's'! Why,.
it's only a place to get news about ships
from ; what should a bit of a gal like you
want to go there for?"

"I don't want to go there, Uncle. But if
it's near Mrs. Wall's, I wish you'd take me
to her."

"Do you want to go back to her?"

"Not to stay, Uncle, only to speak to her."

"What do you want to say to her, Bab?"

"I want to tell her I thought it was good
of her to give Peep and me that milk for
nothing, last morning, when father said he'd
no money left. She was very cross; but she
must have given us that milk for kindness,
and I want to tell her so and thank her."

Uncle did n't answer directly, but only kept staring at me. I heard him say between his teeth, —

" The rummest, the very rummest — " without finishing. Then he began again, " Is there anything partic'ler. you 'd like to have, Bab ? "

" To go to Mrs. Wall's, Uncle."

" Ay, ay, I know that; but I mean any toy, or doll, or gimcrack, to play with ? "

" Yes, Uncle ; oh, yes, Uncle ! There is one thing I should like to have beyond anything in the world."

" Well, out with it, Bab ; what is it ? "

" The old shell ! the speckled shell ! the shell on Mrs. Wall's mantel-shelf ! " I said ; and I could n't help clasping my hands with joy only to think of it.

" A shell ! "

" Yes, Uncle ; the shell that mother used to hold to our ears that we might hear the sound of the sea, where Uncle was always sailing on, — the shell that father liked to hold in his hands, and kept smoothing and smoothing it when he talked to us of mother after she went away to heaven. Oh, if I could have that shell for my very own, Uncle! Do you think I could?"

"We'll see about it, Bab," Uncle said, in a very quiet tone, quite different from the roaring voice he generally talked in.

When I took Peep up to bed that night, I asked him if he would like to go to Mrs. Wall's with me, in case Uncle should take me there.

"No, Bab, I should n't."

"But should you mind being left alone without me here, Peep?"

"No, Bab, not if I should have Ned Carter to play with me while you're gone."

"Then I'll ask Uncle to let Ned come here the day I'm away, Peep."

## CHAPTER III.

S AL had made us up a bed in a room that led from the staircase-landing, on the opposite side to the one where we slept the first night; but it looked on the garden just the same, and I could see the trees, and the grass, and the pigeons quite as well. After breakfast, before Uncle went away to town, Sal asked him whether he wanted her to buy some night-clothes for the children, as they had none of their own, nor any change of linen at all, for that matter, as they'd been brought here in such a hurry, she supposed they'd left their box behind 'em.

"Get what's needful for 'em, Sal, and let me know what there is to pay," said Uncle, as he walked off along the garden-path and slammed the gate behind him.

When I saw Sal putting on her bonnet and shawl, I said, —

"Would you mind letting Peep and me go with you, Sal?"

"What should you want to go for?" she said, in a rather more snappish tone than usual.

"It'd amuse us; we should like to see what it's like outside the garden."

"I dare say; just like you child'n's cur'osity. What d' ye expect to see?"

"I don't know; that's just why we'd like to go, and find out what there is to look at."

"No great thing, I can tell you; just a village like other villages near London, — a shop or two, that's all."

"Oh, but we like to look into shop-windows, especially toyshops, where there are dogs, and horses, and baa-lambs, and wagoner's carts, and windmills, and —"

"Now, don't you think we're going to toyshops. We're going to nothing o' the kind; we're going to a shop for calico and useful things."

" Never mind, we shall like to go there, and see you choose what you 're going to buy."

Sal did n't answer; so I thought she meant not to forbid us. Therefore Peep and I followed her out at the gate, and found ourselves in a pretty road, with houses and gardens on each side; then a green hedge for a little way, with trees and a high wall opposite; and then a few neat shops, into one of which, where there were gay ribbons and bright-colored prints hanging up in the window, Sal suddenly turned. Peep and I watched her buy some calico, and flannel, and socks, and handkerchiefs, till there was a good heap piled up on the counter.

" Sal, would you mind having those things packed up in three parcels instead of one? Peep and I would so like to carry something ourselves."

" Oh, yes, I dare say; and let 'em drop into the mud, or lose 'em, or some mischief. No, thank ye, not I."

" Do, Sal," said Peep. " I should so like to carry home a parcel."

" What persevering toads these child'n are !
Well, do 'em up, miss, in three."

Sal said this to the young woman who was
serving in the shop, and who had been looking at us with a smile. When the three
parcels were packed up, the young woman
picked a pretty ticket of pink and blue, bordered with gold, from off the piece of calico
from which she had cut the yards bought by
Sal, and then cut out a still prettier red-
worked flower, with a long strip of gold edge
from the end of a piece of white muslin, and
putting the two bright scraps into a bit of
paper each, she handed them to Peep and
me, saying, —

" There's something you'd like to have
to play with, wouldn't you ? "

" Oh, yes, thank you ! " Peep and I said,
joyfully, both together, as we stopped behind
Sal for a moment to say this, while she
bounced out of the shop.

" Come along, you dratted child'n ; you
want to come out o' doors with me, and then
you straggle about.  I've no time to lose, if

I'm to be back in time to cook the dinner
for the Cap'n; and I've still got to give
the night-clothes and things to be stitched
and made."

There was a neat little cottage in a small
garden, with a card hanging in the window,
and on the card were big letters that I could
read, "Needlework done here." Into this
cottage Sal went, and she gave the calico and
the flannel to a very pretty young woman
who was there, telling her she wanted 'em
made into shirts and shifts and petticoats of
our size; and she wanted the socks and handkerchiefs marked, all as soon as possible.

"I'm afraid I can't let you have them till
next week," said the pretty young woman, in
one of the sweetest of voices I ever heard;
"my mother is very ill, and nursing her
takes up almost all my time just now; but
if you could give me till next week, I can
promise them faithfully, I think."

"You *think!*" said Sal, in her most snappish tone.

"I mean I'll do my best to get them

finished by the time I promise them," said
the young woman, gently.

"Well, then, Thursday, next week, I shall
expect 'em home without fail, Miss King."

"Where shall I bring them to?"

"To Cap'n Bruff's, Trafalgar Lodge."

I noticed, though I don't think Sal did, that
the gentle-voiced young woman gave a little
start as Sal said this.

"What mark shall I put on the things?"
said the young woman, after waiting a moment without speaking.

"Oh, by the bye, I don't azackly know.
They've queer names, — Bab and Peep; but
I never heard their surnames.  They're niece
and nevvy to Cap'n Bruff, and you can put a
B and a P on their clothes; that'll do to know
'em by.  He brought the child'n home sudden, without a word to me; so how should I
know their right names?"

"A 'B and a P'; very well," was the quiet
answer.  And then we left the cottage and
went home.

## CHAPTER IV.

HE following morning, after break-fast, Uncle said, —

"Peep, you'll find Ned Carter in the garden, ready to have a game with you; and Bab, you and I'll be off to town, to Mrs. Wall's. There's a hack at the door, for I s'pose your little legs couldn't be expected to toddle so far. Sharp's the word, young 'uns. Look out!"

After seeing Peep and Ned Carter happily racing together round the flower-beds, I put my hand in Uncle's and we went to the garden-gate, where a hackney coach was waiting, into which he lifted me, and we drove along, he staring out of the window, silent, as usual.

When we stopped at the door of the house where I had lived ever since I could remember, with father, mother, and Peep, — so hap-

pily while father and mother were not gone
away, — I felt as if I must have cried; but I
thought it might vex Uncle, so I kept in my
tears as well as I could, and went upstairs
with him to the old room I knew so well.
It looked odd and strange though, somehow;
but I turned straight to Mrs. Wall, who had
come into the room with us, and said to
her, —

"I asked Uncle to bring me here to say
thank you, Mrs. Wall, for giving Peep and
me some milk that morning father was taken
away from us, and we had nothing left. So,
thank you, Mrs. Wall."

I went to her, and would have put up my
mouth to kiss her, if she had looked as if she
wished it; but she did n't, so I kept still, looking up in her face, and thinking how cross it
was, and how hard, and how straight her
mouth was, just as I always remembered it.

Uncle brought out from his coat-tail pocket
a lumpy, roundish parcel, and took off the
whitey-brown paper it was wrapped in, saying, —

"I've brought you a little milk-jug, mum, if you'd like to have it. I thought mayhap you would, to remind you of Bab's wanting to come and thank you for giving her and Peep that milk that day. It was a rum start, her wanting to do it; but she's rum altogether, and she did."

"Lauk-a-mussy me! What a to-do about a ha'p'orth o' milk! I give it 'em, o' course, nat'rally, when I know'd they was left starving orphans. As long as their father lived, he allus paid his rent reg'lar for his logdin'; even though he had to pinch hisself and his child'n's stomicks for it, many a time. That I will say for him."

While Mrs. Wall was saying this, I was looking up at the mantel-shelf, where I spied the speckled shell in its old place. Uncle saw my eyes fixed on it, and he walked over to the mantel-shelf, taking the shell into his big hand, where it seemed almost hidden.

"I've been a seafaring man, Mrs. Wall, and I've a fancy for shells from foreign parts. Would you have any objection to parting

4

with this one? What might you want for it,
now?"

"Oh, I don't know; it might be wuth a
matter o' half a crown, or it might be wuth
tuppence. I'm no judge o' shells myself."

"But I am, mum; and I should say a half-
crown would n't be more than you'd get for
it, if you felt inclined to sell it."

"Well, then, you can have it for that."

Uncle put his hand in his trouser pocket,
rattled some silver there, drew out a half-
crown, put it into Mrs. Wall's hand, and taking mine, walked straight out of the room,
and we left the house.

As we drove along in the coach, Uncle
held the shell in his hand loosely, as if he
hardly knew he had it there, for he kept looking out of the window, thinking and thinking, while I kept watching the least scraps of
the shell that peeped beyond his fingers;
then Uncle seemed to remember he had the
shell, for he wrapped it up in the crumpled
whitey-brown paper he had taken off the
milk-jug, and held it covered up in a parcel,

as he turned to look out of the window again.

I did n't like to disturb his thinking, but I could n't help longing and longing to see the shell, and touch the shell, to have it in my own hands. At last I took courage, and got quite close to Uncle, till he felt me against his side. He looked round hastily, as if he'd been wakened out of a dream, and said, with his gruff voice, —

" Well, what is it, little 'un ? "

" If you please, Uncle, if it would n't trouble you much, would you let me carry the shell ? "

" Carry the shell, Bab ? "

" Yes, Uncle; would you mind letting me hold it in my own hands, and look at it, and touch it, and smooth it, as we ride along. I 'll be very careful of it, and won't let it fall and break; and I 'll give it you back as soon as we reach home."

" Give it me back, Bab ? Why, I got it for you; it 's yours, little 'un."

" Mine ! Oh, Uncle ! "

I took it in both hands, — for it was as big and bulgy in one of mine as it seemed small in his, — and I held it close to me, and bent my head over it, that I might n't show my eyes were wet. Uncle turned toward the window again, and I thought he was n't noticing me. So I softly pulled the paper off, and could see and pat the shell as much as ever I liked. And oh, how I did pat it, and stroke it, and whisper to it about father and about mother when they were fond of it too! When I came to thinking about mother, I remembered how she put it to our ears, and told Peep and me about hearing the sea, where Uncle was; and then I lifted it up and listened, and heard the sound of far-off sea waves, that she used to talk of. The shell nearly slipped out of my hand, at the start I gave when Uncle turned suddenly round towards me and said, —

" What are you trying to hear, Bab, — the noise of the sea ? "

I nodded, for somehow I could n't get out any words.

"Where Dolly — where your mother — said I was sailing?"

I nodded again, and Uncle turned away, and looked out of the window as steadily as before.

I looked at his wide back, as I turned and turned the speckled shell round and round in my hands, and I found myself thinking, "I wish Uncle would n't keep his back towards me; I should so like to give him a hug, and tell him how glad I am to have this dear old shell again, and have it for my very own."

But Uncle did keep his back towards me, and his face turned to the coach window; so I began to forget about giving him a hug, and kept smoothing my shell all the way home; and I thought of nothing but the joy of its being mine, — mine for always.

The moment the coach stopped and the door was opened, I nearly fell on my nose, from the hurry in which I tried to get out by myself and show Peep my treasure; but Uncle snatched at my skirts, and said, —

"Hullo, little 'un! Mind yourself! You'll

break your neck, if you fling yourself out of
the hack that way. Wait a bit, till I give
you a heave."

He got out himself, and then lifted me out
in that soft, strong way of his, which always
made me so like to feel myself in his big
arms. I recollect thinking again, even at
that moment, when I was full of showing my
shell to Peep, how glad I should have been if
Uncle had cared to let me give him a good
hug, and thank him for getting the shell for
me; and how pleasant it would be if he gave
me a good hug in return, though his coat-
sleeves were rough and his voice was rougher
still.

I ran to Peep, who was sitting on the
garden-seat, watching Ned Carter dig up one
of the beds that was to be replanted. Peep
started up and flew to meet me; and he was
nearly as glad as I expected, to find I had got
the speckled shell. But he was full of the
games of play he and Ned had had together,
and he could hardly talk of anything else.
Once he broke off to say, —

"Did n't you bring back anything for me, Bab?"

"No, Peep; I 'm sorry, but I could n't buy anything for you, — we 've no money, you know, — or I 'd have brought you a barking toy dog."

"I 'd rather have had a toy wheelbarrow, like Ned's, Bab."

"I only wish I could have bought you one, Peep. But never mind; this dear old shell shall be yours as well as mine; we 'll always call it *ours*."

"No, Bab, thank you; I don't think I care so much about the shell as you do. It 's yours. I 'll tell you what I 've thought. I want Uncle to let me have a wheelbarrow that I can wheel about and put weeds in, and help Ned Carter to weed the garden. You shall ask Uncle for me, Bab; because I don't like asking Uncle, and you don't mind asking him, do you?"

"Well, — no, — not much, Peep; only, just now, when he 's given me this shell, I don't care to ask him for anything fresh; it seems like, like —"

" Oh, if you don't choose to do it for me,
Bab, let it alone; I don't want to *make* you
ask; only if you did n't very much mind
asking, I should like to have a wheelbarrow
beyond anything.   Just as you liked to have
the shell, Bab."

" Yes, Peep; I 'll think about it; and I 'll
try — for *you*, Peep."

" Oh, thank you, thank you, dear, dear Bab !"

And Peep gave me a tight squeeze round
my neck with both his chubby arms, and his
rosy cheek pressed hard against mine, so that
I felt I could even ask Uncle for another gift
so soon after he had made me this one.

When we had done dinner that day, Sal
gave Uncle an account of what she had laid
out in new linen for us; and as she reckoned
up what she had spent in flannel, calico, socks,
and handkerchiefs, my cheeks got very hot
to think how much Peep and I must cost him
to keep us; and I felt still more unwilling to
ask him for the wheelbarrow Peep wanted.
Till, all of a sudden, I heard Sal say, —

" And there 's still the *making* to pay for;

but that won't be till next week, Cap'n, as
Miss King says she can't get 'em done till
then, because her mother's so ill."

I chanced to be looking at Uncle's face,
and I noticed that it got as red as I felt mine
was. His eyes looked quite fierce, too, as he
roared out in his gruffest voice, —

"Miss who?"

"Miss King, Cap'n. She takes in needle-
work; and I've heard say she's a very neat
worker, so I thought I'd give the things to
her to be made and marked."

Uncle hunched himself round towards the
fire with a short grunt, and said nothing more.
Presently he thrust his hand in his trouser
pocket, rattled the silver, and drew out several shillings, sixpences, and half-crowns,
counted out the sum Sal had said she had
paid, and pushed it towards her, saying, —

"There, that's what you've spent; and
you can let me know what the rest comes to,
when you pay it, Sal."

She gathered up the money and bounced
off into the kitchen.

Uncle kept his eyes on the fire, and his back and shoulders seemed wider and rougher than ever, as I looked at them, pondering how I could get courage to speak to him and break through this silence. Then Peep softly nudged me, and whispered, —

"Ask him now, Bab. Oh, I do want the wheelbarrow so much! I want it by the time Ned Carter comes here, and then I can garden with him."

It all of a sudden came into my head that perhaps by helping Ned to weed, Peep might be doing something useful to Uncle in return for so much that he was doing for us; and this gave me courage to blurt out, —

"Uncle, do you mind my interrupting you?"

"Interrupt me, Bab? In what?"

"In thinking. You 're thinking, I suppose, when you keep quiet so long without speaking, Uncle."

"Thinking? Yes, well, I was thinking, sure enough."

"I want to ask you something, Uncle."

" Now, then, little 'un, speak up ; out with it. What is it ? "

" I 've been thinking, too, Uncle ; and I 've thought that if you had a wheelbarrow made for Peep, — smaller, you know, just the size that he could wheel about, — he might help Ned to work, instead of hindering him to play."

" 'Pon my word ! No bad idea ! Well, Bab, I will say this for you, you have the very sensiblest notions in that bit of a noddle of yours that I ever heard tell of in a chit of your age. They 'd do credit to a grown woman, that they would ! I 'll step round to Dick Carpenter's to-morrow, and speak to him about knocking together just such a sized barrow as 'll do for Peep."

" Oh, Uncle ! A barrow ! A real wheel-barrow, for me ! Oh, Uncle, you good, big, kind Uncle ! "

Peep clapped his hands on high, and his eyes sparkled with joy. Uncle stared round at him, then turned again to the fire, and remained some time with his eyes fixed upon

the red-hot coals.  By and by, giving himself a large rough shake, he said, gruffly, —

"Come, it's high time for you young 'uns
to be off to bed, ain't it?"

Upon which Peep and I said "Good-night,
Uncle," and went straight upstairs.

## CHAPTER V.

ALL the afternoon of the next day Peep hung about the garden in a dull sort of way, as if he could n't play or run, or do anything but talk of the wheelbarrow he had been promised.

" Do you think Uncle has thought about it, Bab ? Do you think he remembered to go and order the carpenter to make it, as he said he would ? "

" Yes, Peep, I should think he has; Uncle's always as good as his word, generally better; for he don't *say* much, but he *does* much for us."

" How you keep patting and petting that shell, Bab," said Peep, pettishly. " You seem as if you could think of nothing else ; you can't be attending to what I'm saying about my wheelbarrow."

" Oh, yes, I can ; I do, Peep.   I'm hoping quite as much as you are, that you'll have it soon."

" Do you think the carpenter can get it done by to-morrow, Bab ?"

" Well, perhaps not to-morrow, Peep."

Peep flung himself on the garden-seat, and gave a vexed sigh.

" Next day, then, Bab ?"

" Well, perhaps, next day."

Peep flounced round to his other side, away from me, saying, —

" Oh, Bab !   How tiresome and patient you are !   Do put down that shell and feel angry, with me, about having to wait so long for my barrow."

I laughed a little ; but Peep flounced sharply back again towards me, and said in a furious tone, —

" Don't laugh, Bab ! "

" I won't, Peep.   There, I've put the shell down, and I'm quite thinking about your

barrow. I should n't at all wonder if Uncle
has told the man to be as quick as ever he
can in making it."

" Do you really think so, Bab ? "

And Peep started up and gave me a hearty
squeeze. I was looking over his shoulder as
he did this, and I saw the garden-gate open,
and a man come in, bringing something with
him that made me cry out, —

" Look there, Peep ! Oh, look there ! "

Peep looked round, scrambled off the garden-seat, and ran towards the man, shouting,

" A barrow ! A little barrow ! It 's mine !
It 's meant for me ! "

" Yes, young master," said the man ; " Cap'n
Bruff came to my shop this morning, and
axed me if I could make him in double-quick
time a barrow fit for a little chap under six
year old, and as luck 'd have it, I 'd got this
one ready-made. It was ordered by Sir
James Buckhurst for his little son ; but he
changed his mind for a four-wheeled cart, so
this was left on my hands, an' I let the Cap'n
have it at a bargain. He paid me for it,

there and then, and told me to bring it up here as sharp as I could ; so here it is."

"You see, Peep, I told you Uncle's always as good as his word, and better."

But Peep was too busy wheeling his barrow about, and trying it at once, to notice much what I said.

"Bab, you stoop and pick the weeds and put 'em in my barrow, and then I can do like Ned Carter, and wheel 'em away to the heap."

"Ned stoops and weeds, as well as wheels them away in the barrow, Peep," I said, laughing.

"I told you not to laugh, Bab ; I don't like you to laugh at what I say.  I want you to help me weeding."

"Well, then, I'll wheel the barrow, Peep, and you can stoop for the weeds."

"No, I want to wheel my own barrow, Bab ; if you help me, you must do what I tell you."

I felt very much inclined to laugh again at Peep's grand, ordering way, and he such a little bit of a fellow; but I did n't want to vex, so I set to, picking the weeds as hard as I could.

While Peep and I were busy at this, a big boy came lounging in at the garden-gate, and stopped suddenly to look at us, with his hands in his pockets.

"Who are you?" he asked, bluffly.

"We 're Bab and Peep," I answered.

"Oh, you are, are you? I 've heard of you two, and of father's bringing you to our house. But I 'm home for the holidays now, so I can see what you 're like with my own eyes."

"What, are you 'Master Tom,' that Sal spoke of?" I said.

"Yes, I 'm Tom, — Tom Bruff. I ain't one to stand any nonsense, you know, so I tell you at once you need n't give me any."

"We have n't any to give you," I said.

"Do you mean that for sauce?" said Tom.

"I don't know what *you* mean," I replied.

"Don't you, though? Well, I mean this: I mean to be master here."

"Of course. Why you *are* master, here; you're Master Tom. Sal calls you so, and so do we."

"Oh, then you've talked me over, have you, already?"

"Yes, we wanted to see you; and we hoped you'd come home soon, that we might see what kind of a boy you are."

"Well, you see, now; and you see I'm not one to have his nose put out o' joint with father, or one to put up with any gammon; so just you mind what you're about, you two."

I looked at Tom's nose, and I wondered again what he meant; but I didn't answer. Presently he made a dive into the wheelbarrow, snatched up handful after handful of the weeds we'd collected, and strewed them on the gravel-path, finally giving a kick to the wheelbarrow.

This last rudeness to his dear new barrow made Peep burst out a-crying, and I ran to comfort him.

"Cry, baby, cry. Put its finger in its

eye! If there is a thing I detest, it 's a cry-baby," said Tom, tauntingly.

"Why did you make him cry, then?" I said.

The boy turned on his heel and did n't answer; so I wiped Peep's eyes, and whispered to him, —

" Never mind; when he 's gone away, I 'll help you to pick up the weeds and put 'em in the barrow again."

" But he won't be gone away, Bab; he 'll be staying here, living here, you know. Uncle 's his father, and he 'll keep him at home."

" Perhaps only as long as the holidays, Peep; he 'll most likely only stay here till they 're over, and then go back to school."

Peep cleared up a little at this; but just then I caught sight of Tom, who had lounged over to the garden-seat, where I had left my shell when I went to help at weeding, and saw him take it up in his big fists and begin tossing it up in the air and catching it, like a ball.

" Oh, my shell! my shell! It 'll drop! It 'll break! " I cried.

Tom only laughed a scoffing laugh, and went on tossing up the shell higher and higher.

" Oh, pray don't! pray don't! It 'll get broken! "

" Don't you fret yourself! I sha n't drop it. See here! "

And Tom flung himself down full-length on the garden-seat, tossing up the shell as he lay flat on his back. This brought his head down very low, — so low, that while I was screaming to him and begging him to stop, I did n't notice that Peep had crept round and got quite close to Tom, whose upturned face was just within Peep's reach. Then I saw Peep suddenly bang his little bit of a hand right between the big boy's cheeks.

" You give up Bab's shell! " said Peep, through his ground teeth.

Tom's nose burst out a-bleeding; and I saw in Peep's hand a jagged flint-stone that he had picked up as he crept round.

"Oh, Peep, what have you done? Killed him!"

"I don't care if I have, Bab! Why didn't he let your shell alone?"

"Well done, little Plucky!" shouted Tom, with a loud laugh. "You ain't the cry-baby I took you for at first. I like a chap that sticks up for his sister and won't see her teased. I think I shall take a liking to you, Peep, after all; and here's your shell, Bab. You see I told you true when I said I shouldn't drop it. I'm a tip-top hand at tossing and catching. Here it is, all safe and sound."

"Oh, thank you! thank you, Tom!" I said, as I seized my shell and cleaned it from the blood that had flowed from Tom's nose and smeared its speckled shininess.

When we went indoors, Sal seemed glad to see Master Tom returned; but she soon saw the blood on his face and hands, and spied some specks on my chest, where I had hugged the shell with joy to get it back again.

"What on earth have you all been at, — fighting already?"

She looked so hard at me, and seemed so ready to give me a cuff at the bare thought of my having harmed her Master Tom, that he stepped between her and me, and said, —

"Fighting? Not a bit of it. We're the best o' friends already. My nose came against a flint-stone that set it a-bleeding; and Bab's pinafore and handkerchief got spotted wiping away the blood; did n't it, Bab?"

I could hardly help laughing at Tom's way of putting it, which was true, and yet not quite true. But I thought he meant kindly, and said it to save us from Sal's anger; so I answered nothing, and it passed off. She set some bread and cheese on the table, and put some fruit with it to make a better lunch for Master Tom; saying if she 'd known he was coming to-day, she 'd ha' made him an apple turnover, that she knew he was so fond of.

"Never mind, old gal; you can give it us for dinner, you know; and that 'll come to the same thing, in honor of my lordship's return home for the holidays, you know."

Tom helped the fruit, and cut off the portions of bread and cheese himself, sitting at the head of the table in his father's place.

" Having you there, Tom, seems like having Uncle with us when he 's away," I said.

Tom nodded, and looked pleased.

" Yes, *when he 's away*," said Peep.

" When father 's away, I 'm master here, of course."

" But when he 's at home, *he 's* master ; and I like him to be here," said Peep.

" Are you giving us sauce with the bread and cheese ? " said Tom. " You may like father best for master, but you 'll have to like me next best. If he 's head master, I 'm second master. Understand that, young chap."

" You *must* be master, — always master : you 're Master Tom, you know," I said, laughing.

Tom laughed too, saying, —

" You 're a bright one, you are, Bab. Here, have another apple, — this rosy-cheeked one."

After lunch, Tom sauntered off, saying he was going to take a turn through the village, and look up some of the people he knew there; and while he was gone, Peep and I had some good fun in the garden, playing with the barrow and the shell, after I had helped to pick up the weeds that had been scattered about.

"I'm sorry Tom's come home for the holidays, Bab."

"Are you, Peep? Why?"

"He's so bluff, and so ordering, and so full of his being master over us, Bab."

"Well, I don't know that that much matters, does it, Peep?"

"Yes. I don't like it, Bab. Till he came back, we could do as we pleased all day; and now, perhaps he won't let us."

"We don't know that he won't, Peep. Wait till we see."

"We know already, Bab. I don't mind his being master in helping us to the good things on the table; but I do mind his being master in flinging the weeds out of my barrow, and

his chucking up your shell when you told
him not. He wants to master us because
he 's bigger; and he *can* master us, because
he 's stronger. And I don't like it, Bab."

" Well, he was n't ill-natured when you
made his nose bleed, Peep ; and he was good-
natured when he tried to hide who did it
from Sal."

Peep only grunted, but did n't answer.
Presently he saw Ned Carter come into the
garden, and he ran off to have a game of
play with him, and make him carry him
about pick-a-back. I watched Peep amusing
himself, and was glad he was amused ; but
I felt a little dull after a time, and a little
lonely at having nobody to play with me. I
began to think it a little hard that Peep had
a boy he liked for a playfellow, while there
was no girl I liked to have a game with me ;
and I was getting rather cross and almost
angry with Peep for leaving me by myself,
and I found I was pouting and frowning and
letting myself get into quite a bad humor.
So I got up and fetched my shell, and

brought it out in the garden, and talked to it a little about father and mother; and after a little while, smoothing it and thinking how good Uncle had been to get it for me and give it to me, I did n't feel so lonely; and I could watch Peep playing with Ned without being vexed at all.

## CHAPTER VI.

FEW mornings after this, when I awoke, I found Peep very heavy and sleepy, and unwilling to get up; but after some coaxing he gave way, and let me wash and dress him as usual. Yet he seemed still but half awake; and even when we went down to the breakfast-parlor he looked drowsy, and hardly noticed what was on the table, which he generally attended to a good deal.

"Oh, Peep, here's some honey!" I whispered to him, hoping that would rouse him.

He did for a moment look up, and his eyes sparkled with joy.

Uncle was, as usual, hidden behind his big newspaper; but Tom said briskly, —

"Ay, here's honey, young people! Have some! I'll help you."

He put some on two slices of bread, and passed them over to Peep and me. I thanked Tom, and Peep took his slice as if he liked the thoughts of eating it; but soon I noticed that he put it down on his plate, with only a bite or two taken. Uncle did n't seem to see anything that was going on; and Tom, when his father took his hat and went away to town, put on his cap too, and lounged off for a turn in the village, saying, —

" It 's precious slow here ! "

As neither of them had seen that Peep's cheeks were very red, and that he had eaten no breakfast, I thought it perhaps was not of any consequence; but I could n't help feeling very uncomfortable about him when I saw that instead of going out to play in the garden, as he generally did as soon as we were left alone, he threw himself on the hearth-rug, and said, —

" Oh, I 've got such a pain in my head, Bab; and I 'm so hot, and so I-don't-know-how ! "

" Why do you lie so near the fire, Peep, if you feel too hot ? "

"Oh, I don't know, Bab; I'm too hot, and yet I'm so shivery."

I went and sat down beside him on the rug, and made a pillow for his head on my lap, and felt his red cheek, which was burning like fire !

"How nice and cool your hand is, Bab ! Put it on my forehead and hold it there."

I did, and we sat quite still for a little. I thought very likely Peep was ill, and wished I could do something to help him, and get something to give him, though I could n't tell what. I had a great mind to get up and ask Sal about it; but I knew she would be cross, as she always was, — particularly when we went and troubled her in her kitchen. Besides, I thought if I got up I should disturb Peep, whose head was resting on my knee, and he seemed quieter now since it was there. So I sat and thought and thought, and could not help crying worse than I had been inclined to cry a day or two before when I felt left out from play. That was somehow a cross feeling as well as a sad one; but now it was nothing else but a sad, sorrowful, miserable feeling. I was ashamed now to have half cried then; because I now found how much worse it was to be crying for Peep than to be crying for myself. It was in a confused way that I thought all this; but I did think it, and it made me sob more bitterly than ever. It then came into my head what I once heard mother say, — "When you've nobody to help you, ask God to help you." So I tried to stop sobbing, and said, —

"Do, God, help us! Do, God, pity us! Peep and I have nobody to help us; do you, God, help us!"

While I was saying this the room-door opened, and Sal bounced in to clear away the breakfast-things.

"What in the world are you two idle brats lying there for? Get up with you, this minute, and go and play in the garden, and let's have the house quit of you while I sweep up a bit."

"Hush, Sal, don't disturb Peep; he's quiet

now; but he says his head aches, and I think he must be ill."

" Parcel o' fancies! I've no patience with such nonsense! Ill indeed ! "

She bounced about in her usual way, and made such a dreadful clatter with the breakfast-things that I thought Peep must be waked up by the noise. But he lay quite still, and never even opened his eyes. As I sat watching Sal's bounce-about movements and cross looks, I found myself thinking, " Is this how God helps us?"

Presently there came a ring at the door-bell, and Sal bounced out to see who rang. I heard her voice saying, —

" Oh, it's you, Miss King, is it? Brought home the things, I s'pose. Step in here, and I'll see that they're all right, and pay you at once."

She came into the parlor, followed by the pretty young woman, who opened the bundle she carried, and began counting the linen and socks it contained.

" All right, Miss King. How much do you

make it?  Stop a bit; I'll fetch the money
from the kitchen and be with you directly."

She bounced out, and Miss King looked towards us.  Then she said in her gentle voice,

"What's the matter, dear?  What have
you been crying for?  I see you've been
crying.  What about?"

"Peep's head aches badly, and I'm afraid
he's ill.  His cheeks are so hot and red, and
his eyes glittered so when they were open,
and now he keeps 'em shut, and looks so
lumpish and still."

Miss King came softly across the room, and
knelt down close beside us.

"The poor little fellow *is* ill," she said,
quietly.  "But don't you cry, dear; it will
only disturb him, and you wouldn't like to
do that, would you?  He ought to be in
bed.  The servant had better carry him at
once to bed."

"I'm afraid Sal won't like to do that.  She
don't like trouble, and I always do everything
for Peep myself."

"But you can't carry him up to bed, and he

is not able to walk himself. Stay; if you'll
show me the way, I'll carry him for you."

Miss King lifted Peep up in her arms, —
so gently that he did n't awake, — and I led
the way upstairs. She laid him on the bed,
and put the coverlets lightly round him, and
placed the pillows comfortably under his
head; and as I watched her doing so, it came
into my head, " *This* is the way God helps us.
I did n't expect to have Miss King, but he
sent her to me."

When she had arranged Peep, she turned
to me and said, —

"Now you will have to be his little nurse;
and when you feel inclined to cry, think of
what you can do for your patient, — your
little brother, I mean, — and you'll find it'll
help you not to cry. I would come myself
and nurse him for you; but mother is so ill
I cannot leave her long together. Besides,
it will be good for you to learn to nurse him,
it will keep you from fretting better than
anything else could. Do you understand me,
dear?"

6

She leaned down and gave me a kiss. It was the first kiss I had had from anybody for so long a time, and her voice was so sweet, and her eyes were so gentle, as she stooped towards me, that I felt dreadfully inclined to cry again; but I wouldn't let myself do it after what she had said, so I only nodded.

"Well, then, dear, listen to me, and I'll tell you what you must do to nurse little brother and make him get well soon. You must coax the servant — Sal, I think you called her — to make you some apple-tea or some toast-and-water, and you must give some to your brother every time he says he's thirsty, and even when he doesn't say so, as often as you can. And before I go home I will get you something to give him besides, which will do him good."

"I'm afraid Sal won't like any trouble; and I shall be afraid to ask her."

"No, dear, you won't be afraid, I know, if it is to help your brother to get well. Come downstairs now, for I must hurry home as fast as I can, after bringing you the something to give him which I promised."

Miss King and I went down into the parlor just as Sal bounced up the kitchen-stairs, saying, —

"That dratted butcher-boy kept me so long waiting. But here's your money, Miss King. How much did you say it comes to?"

Miss King told her, and then said, —

"The little boy has a bad, feverish cold, and he ought to have plenty of cooling drinks. I will bring him some medicine from the chemist's, and will be back directly with it, before I return home. I dare say you will be so good as to make some apple-tea or some toast-and-water for him, and his little sister will give it to him."

Sal muttered something about having enough to do without making a parcel o' slops for sick children ; but somehow Miss King's quiet decided manner, taking for granted Sal would do what was needed, made her not say she would n't.

When Miss King was gone, and Sal had

bounced off to her kitchen, I ran upstairs to
Peep. He was still asleep; so I sat by the
bedside, watching him and noticing how
quickly and pantingly he breathed. Then
I slipped down on my knees and begged God
to make him well, and thanked God for
sending Miss King to help us, and asked
God to let me keep from crying, that I might
be a good nurse to Peep.

It was not long before I heard the door-bell
ring again, and Miss King came upstairs with
a small packet in her hand. She opened it
and showed me some tiny folded papers inside,
one of which she also opened, and I saw a
little powder in it. Then she took from her
pocket a screw of paper and a white spoon,
so clean and so pretty-looking, and she
said, —

"I've brought this nice bone spoon for my
clever little nurse, that she may always keep
it by her, ready for putting one of these
powders into it for her brother. See here;
watch me, and you'll know how to do as
I do."

She unscrewed the little screw of paper that had some powdered sugar in it; put some into the white spoon, and then gently shook the powder from the small folded paper on to the sugar. Then she propped Peep a little higher on his pillow, which half awaked him, and then she put the spoon softly between his lips, and he swallowed what was in it.

"I'm so thirsty," he said, in a weak voice.

Miss King was stepping lightly across the room to the water-bottle on the washing-stand, when in bounced Sal with a glass of toast-and-water in her hand, which she gave to her, saying, —

"I've put some apple-tea on to make, but it takes time, so you must wait for that."

"This toast-and-water will do capitally in the mean while, Sal, and thank you for making it so quickly, and so nice and clear," said Miss King's sweet voice.

Sal bounced out again with a grump, and Miss King held the toast-and-water to Peep's parched lips. He drank a good long draught, and then lay back on the pillow again.

"If you have n't strength to lift him up by yourself, dear, when you give him drink, don't take that large glass in your hand, but just dip the spoon into the toast-and-water or the apple-tea, when Sal brings it up, and give him a spoonful at a time, as often as he wishes for some. You will know when to give him the powders by listening for the kitchen-clock, which you can hear where we are. Hark! there it is! listen! And every time it strikes give him one of the powders as you saw me give it to him. Do you understand, my dear?"

There was something in her face, as she looked at me and leaned down towards me, that made me feel she would n't mind my giving her a kiss of my own accord; so I put up my mouth to hers, and flung my arms round her neck, as I answered, —

"Yes, thank you! oh, thank you!"

She kissed me heartily in return, and said, —

"You're a loving, grateful little soul; and such a mite as you are, too! How old are you?"

"I don't quite know; but I think I'm a little past eight."

"And such a good little nurse as you are going to be. I'm sorry to have to leave you; but I *must* go now. I've been so long away from poor mother. Good-by, dear! I shall come to-morrow morning and see how your brother is going on as early as I possibly can. Good-by again, dear."

She nodded cheerfully at me, and ran quickly but very softly downstairs and out of the house.

I found so much to do in putting the powders side by side, and the paper of sugar near them, and laying the white spoon ready at hand, thinking how nice and clean it looked, and how glad I was to have it, instead of being obliged to ask Sal for a silver one to keep upstairs, that by the time she brought the apple-tea I felt not at all inclined to cry, but quite bright and brisk.

"To see the old-fashioned ways of that chit," muttered Sal as she set the jug down and looked at the powders and all the rest spread out neatly on the table. "It 's like playing with dolls' things, that it is! That she should have the sense to make a game out of nursing her brother! Only think! It beats all I ever see or heard on; that it does."

I gave Peep a little of the apple-tea in the way Miss King had told me how, Sal standing by and watching me all the while, with a sort of half-cross laugh.

"One 'd think you 'd ha' been a hospital nuss all your bit of a life, that one would! I s'pose now you 'd like to have some nice smooth water-grool for him instead of dinner to-day, as he won't be very sharp-set for meat, or even pudd'n', if he 's really ill; should n't you?"

"Oh, what a good thought, Sal! Thank you! Oh, yes, I should, very much."

"Then I 'll make you some, for the sake o' the fun; you are such a queer, old-fashioned child ; I never saw the likes of you, not I."

Peep had fallen into a sound sleep, and his cheeks looked much less red and felt less hot by the time I heard Uncle and Tom come home ; so I went down to dinner with them, not much minding having to leave the bedroom.

" Where 's Peep ? " said Uncle, as I came into the parlor.

" He 's not well, Uncle, and can't come downstairs. But he don't want any dinner, and Sal has made me some gruel for him, which is much better."

" All right ; but if he gets worse he 'll want a doctor, and if he does, let me know, and I 'll send for one."

" Oh, I hope he won't get worse, Uncle ; and even if he does, I 'm sure he won't want a doctor, for he don't like 'em. When a doctor once came to see him, he kicked and screamed, and said he could n't bear doctors because he knew they would make him take physic."

Uncle laughed a loud laugh, and so did Tom. Then they began to talk together, and I, longing to be off to my nursing, ate my dinner as quickly as I could and slid off my chair the moment it was finished; then, bidding Uncle and Tom good-night, I ran upstairs.

## CHAPTER VII.

HAD not long heard Uncle leave the house next morning, and Tom soon after also, than there came a ring at the door-bell, and Miss King, with her soft quick step, ran upstairs to me, and asked how Peep had passed the night.

"Very well indeed. He slept a good deal, and only asked twice for something to drink. So I gave him both times some apple-tea, as he seems to like that better than toast-and-water; and both times I gave him a powder."

"Well done, my little nurse! And his hands are nice and moist this morning, and his forehead too, — not dry and hot and feverish, as they were yesterday. So between us, I think we shall have him soon well again. Go on as you did before; only in-

stead of *every time* you hear the clock strike,
give him one of the powders *every other time*
you hear it strike.   You understand ? "

" Yes, Miss King, quite.   And how good of
you to leave your mother so early to come
and see about Peep !   Is she better ?   Did she
have a good night, as he did ? "

" Not so bad a night as she has sometimes ;
she slept a little towards morning, and has
less pain than she has generally.   Poor, poor
mother !   And she 's so good and patient."

I saw Miss King's eyes fill with tears ; but
I could see that she kept them back, and
*would n't* cry.

" Is she very, very ill ? " I asked, in a low
voice.

" Yes, my dear, very, very ill.   I fear she
can never recover.   I fear I *must* lose her."

Miss King held her hands very tightly together, and spoke in as low a tone as I did.

" Lose her ?   How do you mean ?   Do you
mean she 'll not be found some day when you
go home ?   Can she get out of bed and get
away ? "

"No, dear; I mean, I fear she will be lost to me; that God will take her, and that she will go to heaven."

"Ah, yes, as my mother went and my father went — to heaven. And when people go there, I know they never come back. Oh, I *am* sorry for you, Miss King; I *am* sorry for you. But I 'll try not to cry, and I see you 're trying not to cry; because we know it 's bad for Peep and for your mother, now that we have to nurse them, don't we ?"

Miss King stooped down and gave me a kiss, which I returned with all my heart; and after telling me a few things more that I could do for Peep, she ran away downstairs, and I heard the house-door shut quietly after her.

Peep, as Miss King said he would, soon got quite well, and he then ate as heartily as ever; and Tom heaped his plate, and mine too, with good things at every meal, when Uncle was too busy behind his newspaper to notice that our plates were empty. Indeed, Tom grew very kind to us for some time after Peep had been ill; but by degrees I thought

I saw that Tom became what he was at first, and even more cross and bluff than ever.

One day, when it was getting towards the time that Tom's holidays were coming to an end, and I heard that he was soon going back to school, Peep was playing happily with his wheelbarrow at a little distance from the garden-seat on which I was sitting making a little case for my shell with the bit of red-worked muslin given to me by the smiling young shopwoman, and Tom was leaning with his head on his arm upon the back of the long garden-seat at the end farthest away from me. He was very silent; and as much as I could see of his face looked very frowning and red and hot, though it was a cold day, and Tom had been quite still for a long time.

" Are you ill, Tom ? Do you think you 've got a feverish cold, as Peep had ? "

" No. What makes you think I 'm ill, Bab ? Don't notice me. What do you care if I 've anything the matter with me ? "

" Oh, I care a great deal, Tom. And I

think you may be ill, because you have hot red cheeks, as Peep had when he was ill."

" Ill ?   No, not I.   Don't notice me, Bab, I tell you."

" But I must notice you, Tom ; because if you 're ill, you must be nursed, and I would nurse you."

" You, Bab ?   Nonsense ! "

" Oh, but I can nurse, and very well, too, though I 'm so little.   I nursed Peep capitally ; Miss King said so."

Tom turned upon me fiercely, and said, in a rough loud voice, —

" Who ? "

" Miss King.   She taught me how to nurse, and came to see how Peep got on while I nursed him."

" She came here, did she ?   How came I not to know she did ?   I 'd soon have made the house too hot to hold her, and have sent her to the right-about pretty quick, I can tell you."

" What makes you angry with Miss King, Tom ?   Don't you like her ? "

" Like her ?　I hate her ! "

" Why, Tom ? "

" Because — because —　Oh, you would n't understand why I hate her!　How should you ?　Such a young chit as you, how could you understand what makes me hate her, even if I were to tell you ? "

" Oh, but do tell me, Tom ; try to make me understand.　I want to make out why you should hate Miss King, who has been so good and kind to me, and who seems to me to be just what I could love so very much.　And I do love her already ; I feel I do."

" Love her ?　Love Miss King ?　That you would n't if you knew what I know about her.　You'd hate her, as I do.　I've only lately found it out ; but it makes me detest her."

" What is it, Tom ?　Are you sure it's true ? "

" Oh, yes, it's too true ; those who told it me see proofs of it every day."

" But what is it, Tom ? "

" Why, it's just this, and nothing else :

she's trying to get father for a husband. He goes every day to see her, and wants her to marry him."

"That seems as if *he*'s trying to get her for a wife; and that would be very nice, Tom."

"Nice, Bab?"

"Yes; because then she'd come and live here, and I should be very glad, for I love her already; I told you so."

"But I don't: I hate her. I hate step-mothers, and I won't have her for one."

"Can you help it, Tom? Why shouldn't you like to have her for a step-mother?"

"Because all step-mothers are hateful and horrible; and if she were to come here as my step-mother, I'd make her repent it; I'd do all I could to make her life miserable."

"Then it would be *you*, Tom, who would be hateful and horrible, not she."

"There, Bab! I told you you wouldn't be able to understand. Step-mothers are always disagreeable; everybody says so."

"But I don't think, — I *can't* think she would be. Oh, Tom, you don't know how

7

gentle and sweet-voiced and kind Miss King
is!"

"Don't call her 'Miss King' to me, Bab!
I never call her so; I call her Pen Prim.
I've heard of her soft, silky ways, and I call
her Pen Prim, and I shall never call her anything else. And if you care anything for
me, you'll call her Pen Prim, too, Bab, to
please me."

"Why do you call her 'Pen,' Tom?"

"Because her name's Penelope; and as
sure as my name's Tom, I'll never call her
anything but Pen Prim."

"Perhaps you'll have to call her step-
mother, Tom."

"That I won't if I can help it."

"But if you can't help it, Tom?"

"How aggravating you are, Bab! No, I
never will call her so. If father will have
her, — and when he's bent on a thing he
generally has his way, — if he will marry
her, and if I can't help myself in that, at
least I'll never call her anything but Pen
Prim to the end of her days; and I'll not

make her married life too pleasant to her, if she does succeed in getting father for a husband and comes to live here. And if you care for me at all, Bab, you'll promise to worry her just as much when I'm away at school as I should if I were always at home. Come, promise me you will."

"I can't promise that, Tom."

"Then you don't care for me, Bab."

"Yes, I do, Tom. You are not so bluff and gruff to Peep and me now as you were at first, therefore I like you now very much."

"You do, Bab? Well, then, show that you like me, by calling her Pen Prim, and by being as rude as ever you can to her whenever she comes here."

"No, Tom, not even to please you, will I promise that. She has been very good to Peep and to me when he was ill; and I know I couldn't be rude to her, even if I tried."

"But will you try?"

"No, Tom, I won't even try."

"Then you don't care for me, and only pretend to like me, Bab."

I could n't answer any more; and Tom got up from the garden-seat and flung away in a huff, saying, —

"See if I forgive you, Miss Bab!"

And he did n't forgive me; for whenever he spoke to me he called me "Miss Bab." But he hardly ever did speak to me at all, till at last the morning came when he was going back to school, and I felt I could n't bear he should not make it up with me before he went. So after watching him all through breakfast, and seeing he looked sulky and cross still, and kept his face turned from my side of the table, I crept round near to him and said in a low voice, so that nobody should hear, —

"Do say you forgive me, Tom, before you go! You'll be such a long time away, and I don't like you to keep angry with me all that while."

"You can be forgiven, you know, Miss Bab, directly; you've only to promise me to do what I told you."

"But I can't promise, Tom."

"Then I can't forgive you, and I sha'n't either. Don't you think it, Miss Bab. You need n't look up at me in that pitiful way; you 've only to do as I tell you, and then I 'll shake hands with you before I go. If not, I won't. See if I do!"

He kept his word. Even when the hackney-coach came to the gate, and his box was put in, and I stood waiting with the rest, hoping he would shake hands with me at the very last moment, he jumped in without even looking at me, though I was trembling and shaking all over, and could n't keep the tears from rolling down my face. Peep was n't ill, so I could cry without fear of doing him any harm; and I did cry very sorrowfully and long.

"Why, who 'd ha' thought you cared so much for Master Tom as to cry 'cause he 's going back to school," said Sal, sharply. "I fancied you were no such great friends as that comes to while he was here."

I did n't answer Sal; but when she was gone down to her kitchen, and Peep noticed

my red eyes, asking what had made me cry,
I burst out afresh, and said, —

"Oh, Peep! Tom did n't shake hands with
me before he went; he did n't even say,
'Good-by, Bab'!"

"Well, it don't signify, Bab; he's almost
always bluff and surly, and don't care for us
much, you know. Why should he? I'm
sure I don't care much for him; I like Ned
Carter fifty times better than I do Tom.
Ned's always good-tempered and willing to
play with me, while Tom only wants to be
master."

## CHAPTER VIII.

EXT day, just as Uncle had his hat on, ready to go out, Sal bounced into the parlor, saying in quite a screaming voice, —

" I 've heard something, Cap'n, that makes me in such a way I can't a-bear myself! And I must have a few words with you at once, Cap'n, to settle my mind whether it 's true or not. They 're a-sayin' in the village that you 're a-thinkin' o' gett'n' married; and if you are, I must tell you plain I 'm not a-goin' to stay here with a new missus over me. *That* I could *not* stand ! "

" My good girl — " Uncle began.

" Don't ' good gal ' me, Cap'n ; I 'm not a-going to stand havin' a missus here, — no, not to please even you, Cap'n."

" But, Sal — "

"No, Cap'n Bruff, sir, I couldn't hear of stayin', much as I like my place. If a missus is to come to this house, I'd leave at once, and I'd give you warnin' on the spot."

"But, Sal, consider —"

"Don't think it for a minnit, Cap'n; I couldn't, and what's more I wouldn't; so you can think it over, sir."

Sal bounced off, banging the door behind her, and Uncle stood looking at the fire, with his hat still upon his head, but not going out.

I crept near to him, hoping he would notice me; but as he didn't, I put up my hand very gently and touched him on his thick coat-sleeve. He didn't feel me at first, but when I said softly, "Uncle!" he looked down at me, and said, —

"Well, Bab, what is it?"

"Do you want very much to be married, Uncle?"

Uncle got very red; then he laughed, and said, —

"Why do you want to know, Bab?"

"Because, Uncle, if you do, you need n't mind Sal's saying she'll go, need you?"

"Well, Bab, it'll be very inconvenient having no servant to keep things going here a little tidily. And Sal's accustomed to my ways, and knows how I like to have 'em done; and if she leaves me all of a hurry, I should n't be able to get on till I bring home a wife to set things straight for good and all. And I should like to have the place neat and tidy before she comes here, you see, Bab."

"I don't think Sal *is* very neat and tidy, Uncle; is she?"

"Well, I don't know, Bab; perhaps not; but I'm used to her, you see, and that's the fact. Besides, I don't know how I could manage to get anybody else in her place, if she left me suddenly. You heard her say she'd give me warning at once."

"Let her, Uncle."

"Ah, yes; but, Bab, what should we do without her?"

"Very well, Uncle."

" Not very well, Bab ; the place would be
all sixes and sevens, without somebody to
clean up, and cook, and make beds, and all
the rest of it."

" But we could get somebody instead of
Sal, Uncle."

" Could we, Bab, do you think ? Could
we get any one to come at once, if Sal gave
us warning ? "

" Yes, Uncle, I 'm sure we could. I think
I know somebody who 'd be quite glad to
come and be servant here directly."

" Bab, my little woman, I always said you
were the very rummest child I ever knew for
your age ; and here you are, making me feel
as if you were quite a comfort and a clever
little housekeeper, a wise grown-up person
to consult with, and to help me at a pinch.
Well, what about this servant-girl you think
would be glad to come to us ? "

" Why, Uncle, I heard Ned Carter say the
other day that his sister Sue wanted to get
a new place, for the one she has just left was
a very hard one, and they were very cruel

to her; and he says he would be glad to have
her where they'd be kind to her and not
work her too hard. And here she'd have an
easy place and be quite happy, you know,
Uncle."

"So she would, Bab; with such a little
mistress as you at first, and with such a mistress as — Well, I must n't stay any longer,
I must be off to town; so good-by, Bab."
And Uncle suddenly hurried away.

Luckily this was one of Ned Carter's days
for coming to do some gardening; so I went
to him the moment he entered the gate, and
said, —

"Did n't you say your sister Sue wants a
place, Ned?"

"Yes, little miss, she do."

"Don't you think she'd like to come here,
Ned?"

"Like, little miss! She'd be ready to fly
out of her skin wi' joy, if she could get *this*
place! But then there's Sal; mayhap *she*
would n't like it at all."

"Never mind Sal, Ned. You tell your

sister to come up first thing to-morrow morning, before Uncle is off to town, and he 'll speak to her about coming here."

"Lord love you, miss, to be sure I will. Sue 'll be ready to jump out of her skin, that she will."

When Uncle came home that evening, and had finished dinner and was sitting over the fire, he called me over to him, away from Peep, who remained at table, very busy play-ing at boats with some large walnut-shells that he had saved from dessert.

"Well, little woman, let's hear what you've done about another servant-girl. Ned was here to-day; did you speak to him?"

"Yes, Uncle; and I told him to tell Sue to step up and speak with you to-morrow morn-ing about coming here at once. He says she 'll jump out of her skin to get such a place."

"Upon my word, Bab, you 're a capital manager already. But you women, if you 're ever so young, seem to be good at managing a house a sight better than us men, if we 're ever so old."

Uncle fell into his usual habit of staring at the fire and saying nothing for a long while. At last he seemed to wake up, and said, —

"Ring the bell, Bab!"

I did so; and Sal bounced into the room with, —

"Well, Cap'n?"

"This morning, Sal, you threatened to give me warning. Now *I* give *you* warning. There's a month's wages besides what is owing to you up to to-night; and to-morrow you go."

"Cap'n!"

"To-morrow you go!"

"Well, I never! Sent off at a word in this way!"

"You threatened to go off at a word, and without caring whether it put me to an inconvenience or not; so to-morrow you go."

"And pretty early, too; you see if I don't, Cap'n! I'll just make your breakfast for you, and after that I shall pack up my alls and be gone, and you may shift how you can

for your dinner.   If you were starving for it,
I would n't cook it; and I 'll never set foot
in this house again; there!"

"Mind you never do," said Uncle, as Sal
bounced out of the room.

"A good riddance of bad rubbish," I heard
him mutter.   Then he turned to me and
said,—

"You clever little woman, you got rid of
her for me.   What would you like me to
bring for you from town, Bab?   Would you
like to have a doll?"

"Oh, Uncle!   A doll!"

"Yes, a wax doll,— a big pretty one, with
baby-clothes on."

"Oh, Uncle!   A doll!   A beautiful doll!"

I stopped suddenly, thinking of something.

"Well, Bab, what is it?   Is there anything
you 'd like still better than a doll?   If there
is, out with it."

I felt very odd and very shy, and could n't
say anything for a moment.

"Well, little woman, speak up!   What
is it?"

"Uncle, there's one thing I should like even better than a doll. I should like you to let me give you a kiss, — a hug. I've often wanted to do it; but I — but you —"

"Of all the rum — To give me a hug, — a rough, big bear like me? Are you sure, Bab, you want to kiss me?"

"Very much, Uncle."

"Well, then, kiss me, little woman."

I stood on tiptoe and put both my arms round his neck, and pressed my lips among his great rough beard and whiskers, just where I found a little bit of cheek.

"Thank you, Uncle, for all you've done for Peep and me!" I whispered.

"All? It ain't much; and I have n't been able to take very good care of you, or see to you much. But perhaps soon — perhaps when I bring home a wife, she'll help me to understand how to do better for you."

"Yes, Uncle. Miss King."

Uncle started and stared at me.

"What do you know about Miss King, Bab?"

" She came here while Peep was ill, Uncle, and taught me how to nurse him; and he got well sooner than I think he would have done if she had n't helped me. She was so good and so gentle, and I felt so thankful to her, that when I chanced to hear you were going to marry her, I thought what a good thing it would be, for I loved her already."

Uncle put his big arm round me and drew me on to his knee, and gave me such a kiss that I was even more glad than when he let me kiss him; because then he did n't seem much to care to have a kiss, but now he seemed to care very much.

" You 're right, my little woman; she is good and gentle, and one to love the moment you see her. You 're right, my little woman, my dear, rum little Bab."

Uncle gave me a hearty squeeze, and then began staring into the fire again; but he held me sitting on his knee, with his big warm arm tight round me still. So I liked being kept there ever so long, without his speaking to me or I to him. And after that

evening, whenever Uncle had anything quiet
to say to me or I to him, he used to make
me sit on his knee while he told it me or I
told it him.

Next morning Sal bounced about more
than usual, sniffing and grumping, and setting down the things on the breakfast-table
with a bang. But Uncle did n't take any
notice of her or say a word to her; and she
said nothing to him, till she came up with her
bonnet and shawl on, and said, —

" Well, I 'm going, Cap'n, and it 's to be
hoped you won't miss me."

" It 's to be hoped not, Sal."

" See if you don't, though, Cap'n, when it
comes to dinner-time, and you come home
and find no vittels on the table; that 's
all."

Uncle did n't answer, so I said, —

" Sal, why do you speak as if you were
spiteful against Uncle, when you 've made
such good dinners for him all this time, and
got us a bed ready, and some night-clothes for
Peep and me to put on when we came here

that first night? Thank you for *that*, at least, Sal; and good-by, Sal."

"Good-by, Sal!" said Peep, very briskly.

Sal gave a sort of half laugh, half snort, as she said, —

"I shall send for my box this arternoon;" and then flounced straight out of the room and out of the house.

Not long after, there came a ring at the door-bell, and I slipped out to open it, and, as I expected, there was Susan Carter. I brought her into the parlor, and said, —

"Uncle, here's Sue."

He asked her if she had come to stay at once, and she, dropping a courtesy, said, —

"Yes, Cap'n, if I may."

"Yes, my girl, you may."

Then he spoke to her about wages, when she dropped another courtesy, and he said, —

"My little missy here 'll tell you all about my ways and my hours, and what I like to have for breakfast and for dinner, and — and all the rest of it; won't you, Bab?"

"Yes, Uncle."

He put on his hat and went out at once;
while I took Sue downstairs to the kitchen,
and then upstairs to the bedrooms, and
showed her all about the house. Then I
said, —

"The butcher-boy generally comes here
about eleven o'clock, Sue; and Uncle likes
to have beef oftener than any other meat, so
you can order some for to-day to begin with."

"And Uncle often has a pudding or a pie,
Sue," said Peep.

"Can you make puddings and pies, Sue?"
I asked.

"Oh, yes, miss; and very light crust too."

"That's a good thing!" said Peep. "You
can make a pie or a pudding every day,
Sue."

"Shall I, miss?"

"Yes, I think you may, Sue."

"Does the Cap'n like his meat under-done
or much done, miss?"

"He generally has the brown outside slice,
Sue; but he likes the inside to just have the
gravy in, — juicy, you know."

" I understand, miss."

" And, Sue, you may sometimes give us apple dumplings or pancakes, for a change," said Peep. " And, Sue, I like boiled paste better than baked paste, so you can give us puddings oftener than pies."

" Very well, sir.   Shall I, miss ? "

" Yes, Sue."

Just then there came a loud ring at the door-bell, and we heard shrill whistling outside.

" That's the butcher-boy," said Peep. " Order ribs of beef to-day, Sue; and give us a roly-poly pudding afterwards. Oh, and put plenty of plums in it, Sue."

" Yes, sir," said Sue, as she flew off to open the door and give the butcher-boy his orders.

" Some day, Sue, you may tell him to bring steaks and kidneys, and you can make us a beefsteak pudding," said Peep, when she came back ; " and that day you can give us pancakes, you know."

" Yes, sir.  What time does the Cap'n dine, miss ? "

" Generally about five, Sue ; but sometimes
he 's a little later, so you 'll have to manage
and keep the meat hot, ready for any hour
Uncle comes home."

" I understand, miss."

" And he always breakfasts at nine ; therefore it must be ready exactly then, because
he goes out directly after."

" Yes, miss."

" And, Sue, Uncle likes to have all sorts
of things on the breakfast-table, — sometimes
jam, sometimes honey, sometimes marmalade,
sometimes buttered toast, sometimes hot rolls,
sometimes bloater-herring, sometimes eggs
and bacon, sometimes chops, sometimes —
sometimes — oh, I 'll think of more things
presently ; but you may often have hot rolls,
Sue," said Peep.

" Very well, sir."

" And, Sue, be sure you have Uncle's coat
brushed and his boots blacked and brought in
the first thing, so that I may set them by the
fender, ready for him to put on before he
goes out; and you 'll have to take in his

paper before breakfast and bring it into the parlor: the newspaper-boy comes round at eight."

" Yes, miss."

" And I'll show you the store-cupboard, Sue; where the tea and sugar and the pepper and salt and the raisins and currants and spices and jam-pots are kept; and the corner where the candle-and-soap box stands; and the closet where the mops and brooms and brushes are put; and I should like you to buy a few neat little white covered jars for the store-cupboard, Sue, so that the spices and the pepper and the salt may be kept nicely, as mother used to keep them, instead of screwed up in bits of paper, as Sal used to keep them."

" I understand, miss."

And Sue showed that she did understand; for not long after she came, the house was swept and scoured as it had not been for many a day. Every room was like a new pin for neatness and cleanliness; she kept everything in its place and thoroughly dusted;

she bought new house-cloths and glass-and-china cloths instead of the rags Sal used and thought good enough; for Uncle gave Sue a good supply of money in hand, and bade her not spare in getting anything the house wanted. She not only kept it in good order, but she cooked capitally; and Uncle said he had not eaten better dinners he did not know the time when, and Peep enjoyed himself completely. She was very brisk and good-tempered too, and flew about from morning till night, singing at her work, and always ready to have a chat with Peep and me, or to do any little job we wanted at any odd moment. She was fond of chatting; but she never left off from what she was about while she chatted. She used to flit from room to room all the time she talked, if she were making the beds or doing any house-work; so that Peep and I had to follow from place to place as we listened to her stories and village gossip, of which she had an endless store. She seemed to know everybody and to have heard everything; and she amused us very much by the odd way she had of telling about the people living near.

Peep and I had plenty of amusement now, and never felt dull, as we had sometimes felt when we first came to Uncle's house; and besides, he brought me from town a beautiful large wax-doll, dressed in long clothes, like a baby, and with a pretty baby's cap on its head, all of which were made so that they could be taken off and put on again; therefore I could dress and undress my dolly as often as I pleased.

## CHAPTER IX.

HAD often wished I could go be-
yond the garden-gate and see more
of what was outside Uncle's house,
and I thought it would be so pleasant and free if Peep and I could do so by
ourselves; but as long as Sal was there and
forbade us, we had never dared to venture
out. Now, however, that Sue let us do just
as we pleased, I asked Peep if he would n't
like to come for a walk with me.

"What a capital thing, Bab! Let's go at
once."

It was a fine afternoon, and not very cold;
but above the low light at the edge of the
sky there were some darkish clouds and
streaks, with a mistiness between. We very
much enjoyed our ramble through the village;
looking in at the shop-windows and into the

pretty bits of gardens that were in front of the houses and cottages, until we got to the end of the village, and I thought of turning back. But Peep wanted to go up a steepish hill there was, as he said he should like to see what there was at the top; so we went on and on, till we felt rather tired and longed to sit down and rest. Fortunately, under some trees at the top of the hill there was a nice wooden seat; but sitting upon it, with her frock wide spread out and a smartly dressed doll beside her, was a little girl, about my age, who only stared at us when we looked longingly at the seat. It was long enough for us all to have sat upon it; but the silk skirts of the little girl and those of the doll took up all the room. Near to the little girl stood a young woman, who leaned her back against the tree under which the seat was placed. Seeing that nothing but a hard stare met our longing looks, Peep and I moved closer to the bench and tried to edge ourselves on to it; but the little girl frowned, and said in a sharp voice, —

"Take care, you'll brush against my doll."

"Then take it off the bench; Bab's tired, and wants to sit down, and so do I," said Peep.

"I shan't."

"You must; we're tired and want to rest."

"What do I care?"

"You're a rude girl."

"I'm not a girl; I'm a young lady."

"You're not; young ladies don't speak so rudely. Make room."

"I shan't, I tell you."

Peep didn't answer her any more, but stepped forward and swept the doll right off the seat on to the ground.

"Oh, it'll be all dusty! Oh, its silk clothes will be spoilt!" cried the little girl.

I picked up the doll, brushed the dust off, and said, —

"I don't think it's hurt; it looks as bright and beautiful as ever."

"Yes, isn't it a beauty? Pa gave it me on my last birthday, and I don't think there ever was such a handsome doll. Look at its clothes, — all real silk, and satin, and velvet."

The little girl took the doll and held it before herself and me, while she drew her own skirts towards her, and cleared enough space on the seat for Peep and me, where we sat down and rested.

"Its dress is rich silk, its mantle is thick satin, and its hat is real silk velvet, with a lovely curly feather. Just look! Did you ever see such a beautiful doll?"

"Well, it's beautifully dressed; but I think my own doll, that Uncle gave me, is prettier."

"Oh, impossible! Never was such a handsome doll as mine," said the little girl, with a toss of her head. "I know there is n't! There *can't* be! Why, pa gave more than two guineas for it."

"I don't know how much mine cost; Uncle did n't tell me; but it's very, very pretty, and I love it dearly."

"Well, I don't *love* my doll; but I care for it a good deal, it's so handsome and so

beautifully dressed. Pa never spares price
when he gives me anything, and he gives me
lots of presents."

" Does he ? " said Peep.

" Yes, he 's very rich ; he is called the rich
Mr. Botterby. And I shall be rich some day.
I shall be an heiress, Ledwick says."

" What 's an heiress ? Somebody who gives
herself airs ? " asked Peep.

" No, stupid ; somebody who has lots and
lots of money to do as she likes with. Here,
Ledwick, take my doll and hold it carefully."

" Yes, Miss Botterby."

" Don't you carry your doll yourself ? Bab
always does," said Peep.

" Who 's Bab ? "

" She 's my sister."

Peep pointed to me, and Miss Botterby
stared at me again. Then she said, —

" Ah, it may be all very well for your
sister to carry her own doll ; most likely she
has n't a servant to carry it for her ; but I
have. Ma never lets me go out without

Ledwick to attend me. You see, I'm the daughter of the rich Mr. Botterby, and it would n't do for me to go about alone, like a nobody."

"Are you a somebody?" asked Peep.

"Of course; and ma don't approve of my mixing with nobodies. Who's your pa and ma?"

"We have n't got any. They're gone to heaven. We have only Uncle now."

"Who's he?"

"Captain Bruff; we live with him."

"A captain, is he?"

"Yes."

"He's the Uncle who gave me the doll I told you of; I'll bring it to show you some day," I said.

"You can if you like; but I know it can't be nearly so beautiful as mine. Has it real silk clothes?"

"No; it has white baby-clothes."

"Oh, muslin, or linen, or calico; it can't be so handsome as mine."

"But it's very pretty, and the clothes can

take off and on, and they can wash. Silk
ones can't, you know."

" Oh, well, 1 don't mind that. If my doll's
dress had been spoilt when it was tumbled
into the dust, I could have asked pa to buy
me a new one. He never minds expense."

" He seems to be a very kind papa."

" I don't know about 'kind.' He sometimes rows up awfully; but he don't mind
spending money."

" Don't you think, miss, you 'd better be
going home ? " said Ledwick. " It 's getting
dark ; and you know your ma does n't like
you to be out after dark, she 's so afeard of
your taking cold, you know."

" Oh, yes ; 1 know how she fusses over me.
Well, let 's go home. And if you like to
come here again some day," she said, turning
to me, " to show me your doll, you can. I
often come here when the weather 's fine ;
this walk 's just a nice distance from where
1 live, — Botterby House, you know, — and
this seat is nice to rest upon before I go
back."

We took a hasty leave of her, Peep and I setting off to run downhill, as evening was fast coming on and the clouds were thickening over the sky. As we passed through the village I looked up at the window of the cottage where I knew Miss King lived, and wondered whether her mother was any better. I saw a light behind the white curtain-blind, and wished I could go in and ask; but it was getting so late that I hurried on, hoping to be home before Uncle returned to dinner.

We were there in such good time that I had plenty for putting his slippers near the fender, and setting his chair close by the fire ready for him just as we heard his ring at the bell. He seemed more than ever inclined to be silent and busily thinking that evening; so I did n't talk to him, but sat with Peep, looking over the funny figures in a picture-book that Uncle had brought us from town.

We were very glad of this picture-book, as well as of a box of bricks and a Noah's ark that he had lately given us, for several days after this; because next morning we found the garden was all white with snow, and we could not get out of doors for nearly a week. We used to see Ned Carter come the first thing in the morning to sweep a path through the snow from the house-door to the garden-gate, for Uncle to go out by; but no gardening could be done all that time, so Peep had no amusement except indoors; though he was n't dull, playing with his toys, or I either, dressing and undressing my doll and putting her to bed in the cradle which Uncle had also given me for her. But I sometimes thought of Miss King, and wished very much I could have gone and seen her and asked her how her mother was; which I should have done, if it had not snowed so hard every day. At last I thought of asking Sue if she had heard anything of Mrs. King.

"Lor', yes, miss; I 've heard she 's as bad as bad can be, and ain't expected to last long. Poor Miss King takes it to heart dreadful, and sits by her mother's bedside night and day; never leaves her for a single instant. It 's wearing herself out, she is;

9

and a good daughter she is, that's the truth. And everybody says so too."

"I wonder whether Uncle knows she's wearing herself out."

"Lor' bless you, yes, Miss, to be sure he do. There's not a day he misses calling to know how Mrs. King's a-going on; he's done so for many a day; but Miss King can hardly spare him a moment away from her mother, and only just sees him, and tells him she's no better, and then runs away upstairs again. I know it; for the blacksmith's forge is just opposite the cottage where they live, and the blacksmith's daughter, Polly Trebbitt, is my great friend, and is the best of friends too with Bet, the servant-gal at Mrs. Hodgkin's, where Mrs. and Miss King lodge; so Polly tells me all about them. They've been gentlefolks, you see, miss, and have come down in the world; so Miss King has done needlework for her living, and has kept her mother comfortable ever since with her own hands."

"That must be very comfortable for herself, Sue."

" Yes, miss, to be sure it is ; for, in course, her mother kept her while they were well off, and she's comforted to be able to keep her mother when they're badly off."

" And Miss King sadly wants comfort now, Sue, if her mother is so ill, so very ill, that she can't recover. I wish I could go and see her, and try to give her all the comfort I can. She was very good to me, and comforted me very much when Peep was so ill."

" Well, miss, when the snow gives over, you can go and see her, you know."

" So I can, and so I will, Sue."

The next morning, to my great joy, there was no snow falling, and I saw Ned Carter, after sweeping the paths, begin to do a little digging. As soon as Uncle was gone to town, Peep and I ran into the garden, and bade Ned " good morning " before going out of the gate, as I meant to walk straight to Miss King.

" 'Morning, little miss ; 'morning, little master," said Ned, tugging the lock of hair on his forehead. " Bad news in the village. They say that Mrs. King died last night, and that her poor daughter has lain in a dead faint ever since. They're afeard she'll follow her mother in no time, if she ain't kept quiet as quiet can be."

"Then it would n't do for me to go to her, I suppose, Ned?"

"Lor' bless you, miss, it'd be as much as her life's worth to go and bother her now."

"But I would n't bother her, Ned. I would only go and kiss her on tiptoe, just as she lies, and it would n't disturb her, for I would n't even speak one word to her — not even in a whisper."

"I don't know, miss; I doubt you would n't be let to see her. Doctor was called in by Mrs. Hodgkin before light this morning, and he gave strict orders as not a soul but herself was to go a-near her till she come out of her faint. Mrs. Hodgkin is a good kind woman, and she'll see to her herself meantime."

All day long I could think of nothing but Miss King, excepting of Uncle, who I felt sure must be very sorrowful about her. So, when

he came home that evening very late, and
looking as if he did not know what he was
about, or what was on the table, all dinner-
time, I took courage to go to him when he
threw himself into his chair near the fire, after
Sue had taken away the cloth.

I seated myself on his knee, and put my
hand softly on his breast, and said, as gently
as I could, —

"Uncle, I know what you are grieving
for."

"Do you, my little Bab?" he said, in a
dreamy kind of a way.

"Yes, Uncle. You are afraid Miss King
has worn herself out nursing her mother, and
won't be able to marry you. But I think it
must have been such a comfort to her, that
when once she comes out of her 'dead faint,'
she'll not be worn out at all, but perhaps be
the better for having done what she knew she
ought to do; and that ought to comfort you,
oughtn't it, Uncle?"

"It does comfort me, little one; and you
comfort me, my rum little Bab. You talk

to me like the queer little sensible creature
I've always found you; so sensible, that
I'll tell you what I have done, and I think
you'll understand it, bit of a creature as you
are. When I called there this morning — as
I do every morning, you must know — "

"Yes, I know, Uncle."

"You do, Bab? Why, I never said anything to anybody about going there. However, when I went there this morning and
found how it had been with my darling, I
took the matter into my own hands, and acted
for her, as she could n't act for herself. I look
upon her as my wife and upon myself as her
husband, — I have done so ever since she
promised to marry me — "

Uncle said this as if he were half talking
to himself; and, after breaking off for a moment and looking into the fire in his old way,
he went on, still seeming to say it half to
himself, half to me.

"She would never hear of marrying me
as long as her mother lived, lest the change
might hasten her end; so I waited patiently,

to please her. But this morning, when I saw her lying there speechless, just come to after her long swoon, and the doctor standing by, I told him all the truth; said I considered her mine already, and meant to make her my wife as soon as possible. He said I was quite right, and gave me hope that she would soon be herself again; but made it a condition that she should be kept perfectly quiet, and see nobody for the next few days."

"Not even me, Uncle?"

"Not even you, little Bab. Not even me, my little comforter Bab. I mean to keep myself from fretting to see her, by busying myself about her mother's funeral, so as to have it properly and quietly over by the time my darling is herself again. Then, one of these fine mornings I shall take her to some quiet church in London, where we'll get married together; so that I can carry her away for a week or two to the seaside place where she was born, and set her up again in health and strength before bringing her home here."

"Oh, that is a good plan, Uncle!"

I said this to keep on comforting him; therefore I did not tell him how glad I should have been if the wedding could have been in our own pretty village church, where I could have seen him and Miss King married, and Peep and I could have enjoyed the gay sight and pleasant holiday.

## CHAPTER X.

ALL took place as Uncle had planned, and the morning came when he went away to be married. Though it was a bright sunny day, the house looked rather dull, and even in the garden I felt a little dull too, thinking we should not see Uncle coming up the path to dine at home with us that evening; so I asked Peep if we should take a walk together. He joyfully said yes, and I ran to fetch my doll, in case we should chance to meet with Miss Botterby, as I had promised to show it to her.

When we reached the top of the hill, there was nobody on the seat under the tree, so Peep and I had it all to ourselves.

"I'm glad that girl's not here," said he.

"Why, Peep?"

" Because she 's rude, and takes up all the room."

" But she made room for us at last."

" Yes, when I made her make room by pushing off her doll."

" Oh, Peep, you should n't have done that ! *That* was rude; and you might have spoiled it or broken it."

" Suppose I had, her pa would have bought her another; you know she said so. How fond she seems to be of showing off about his riches ! That 's another piece of rudeness in her, as if she wanted to show how much more money they have in their house than other people have in theirs. I don't like her, and I 'm glad she 's not here."

" Well, I 'm sorry; I wanted to show her my doll."

" She would only say it is n't so grand as hers."

" Never mind if she did. I should always like mine best."

" The only thing I should like her to come for, is because she 'd find us here

first, and we'd not make room for *her* this
time."

"Oh, Peep, then you would be as rude as
she was."

Peep did n't answer this, but began shuffling his feet among the dust of the path as
he sat, and seemed to be thinking of what I
said.

Presently I saw coming round the corner
of the lane which turned off from the road at
the top of the hill, Miss Botterby and her
maid Ledwick, who walked a little behind
her, carrying her doll.

"Oh, how lucky! Here she is! And she
has brought her doll with her. How lucky!"

I ran to meet her; but Peep kept his place
on the seat, still shuffling his feet among
the dust and gathering it up into little
heaps.

"Oh, you've brought your doll, as you
promised, I see," said Miss Botterby, as she
and I sat ourselves down. "It's a nice large
doll, and has a very pretty wax face and
arms, and looks exactly like a real baby.

But what a pity it has n't a hat and a mantle on! Mine has, you see, when I take it out of doors."

"Babies don't wear hats and mantles," said Peep.

"But they wear hoods and long cloaks, though."

"Bab can ask Uncle to get a hood and cloak for her doll, if she likes. He always buys her anything she asks for."

"Is your Uncle rich?"

"I should think so! He gives us lots of toys, and lots of good things to eat. He lets us have jam and honey and marmalade and pies and puddings, and he gave me a beautiful real wheelbarrow."

"A wheelbarrow! What a toy! Only fit for a gardener's boy!"

"I like it; and I 'm a gentleman's boy, — a young gentleman."

"Are you?"

Miss Botterby kept her eyes fixed upon Peep for some moments. Then she turned to me and said, —

" When your Uncle buys you a hood and
cloak for your doll, you can come up to Botterby House and show it me properly dressed
for going out; I know ma won't mind your
coming to see us, though she's very particular what little girls and boys I make acquaintance with and invite to our house."

" I don't think I shall ask Uncle to buy me
a hood and cloak for my doll."

" Why not?"

" Because he gives me so many things of
his own accord, that I don't like to ask him
for any. It seems like — like — "

" Encroaching, she means," said Peep.
" Bab often says mother used to tell her it
was not right to be encroaching."

" Well, if you don't like to ask your Uncle
to give you the going-out things for your doll,
I'll tell you what I'll do. I'll let Ledwick
take its measure, and I'll give her some white
cashmere and white satin to make a splendid
hood and cloak for it. I'll get ma to buy me
as much as will be enough to make them,
— I know she will, — and you can come up

to our house and fetch them when they're
made; and then you can see what a beautiful
place we've got, — what handsome furniture
and what fine grounds we have at Botterby
House."

"Oh, how very kind! That will be nice!"

While Ledwick was measuring my doll's
head and round its shoulders and its length,
a little girl in a blue frock and a straw hat,
with a little boy in a sailor's suit, came up the
hill and stopped still, looking at us.

"Let's ask them if they'd like to sit
down," I whispered to Miss Botterby.

"You can, if you like," she answered.

Peep had already slipped off the seat and
offered his place to the little girl in the blue
frock. I gave mine to the little boy who
was with her.

"If we were to squeeze a little and sit
close," said Peep, "there'd be room for us
all."

"My frock would get rumpled if we sat
too near each other," said Miss Botterby.

"Oh, never mind your frock for once in a

way," said Peep, hunching himself on to the edge of the seat at the end farthest from her and close to the little girl.

"Then *you* sit next me," said Miss Botterby to me. "Ma's very particular who comes too near me and is too intimate with me, and I like you better than these children; I don't know who they are, and I seem to know you quite well already."

"What a nice sweet face the little girl has, and what a pretty frock she has on!" I whispered in return.

"It's only common stuff," said Miss Botterby; "and her straw hat is as coarse as coarse can be.  Mine is the finest chip."

She had not lowered her voice as I had, so that all heard what she said.

"If it's only coarse straw, it's a very pretty shape, I think," said Peep, looking up at the hat next him; "and the fine chip one is the ugliest shape I ever saw."

"But chip is much handsomer than straw, and costs more, and everybody would rather wear a chip hat than a straw one if they could afford it," said Miss Botterby, tossing her head.

"I would n't," said the little girl in the blue frock.

"Then you 're a silly thing," said Miss Botterby.

"She ain't silly!" said the little boy, looking up suddenly with flashing eyes across me at Miss Botterby.

"What's that written in gold letters on the ribbon round your hat?" said she, staring at him in return.

"Can't you read?" he said. "Why, they 're big plain letters that anybody can make out."

"Perhaps she can't read," said Peep.

Miss Botterby got very red, and did n't answer. Peep laughed, and said, —

"Why, even I, little as I am, can read those big printing-letters. They spell 'The Terrible.'"

"Quite a good name for him, I declare!" said Miss Botterby. "He looked as if he could have eaten me, just now."

"It is n't his name, it 's the name of his ship," said Peep.

"Oh, indeed! But I should think he 's too young to have a ship."

"I mean the ship he 's supposed to belong to when he 's got on his sailor's suit. Of course it 's not his own name."

"What is his own name?"

"I don't know. What is your name?" said Peep, suddenly, to the little boy.

"Jamie."

"Ah, that 's your Christian name," said Miss Botterby; "but what 's the name of your father and mother?"

"Sir James and Lady Buckhurst," said the little boy, quietly.

Miss Botterby drew back as if she had been suddenly slapped. After a few moments she said, —

"I 'm sure I beg your pardon; I took you for quite poor children, — such plain clothes — no maid with you. Are you allowed to walk out by yourselves?"

"Our old coachman is with us; but he had

to call at the forge about shoeing the horses, so Jamie and I walked up the hill, knowing he would soon overtake us," said the little girl in as quiet a tone as her brother's.

" Really, Miss Buckhurst, if I'd known — '

Seeing that Miss Botterby stopped, as if at a loss what to say, Miss Buckhurst looked at the two dolls and said how beautiful they were.

" Which do you like best ? " asked Miss Botterby.

" I like them both very much ; but I think the baby-doll is perhaps the nicest to have, it's so natural, and must be so pleasant to play with.  Yes, for my own, I should like a baby-doll certainly best."

" Have n't you got a doll, then ? "

" No ; my father says he has not money enough to afford many toys for us.   He lately gave Jamie a strong cart, because he said it would do for us both to play with, and that it would last a long time."

" Then, after all, you are poor ? "

" Well, yes ; we are not rich, I believe.

My mother often says so, and teaches us to be careful and never wasteful."

" Oh, well, *my* pa and ma are very rich. He 's called ' the rich Mr. Botterby,' and we live at Botterby House. Would you like to come and see it some day ? I 'm sure ma would n't object to my inviting you; and we should be very glad to see you there and show you over the place."

" I will ask my mother if she will let me come. Oh, there 's Stubbs," said Miss Buckhurst, as the old coachman came up the hill towards us. She wished us all quietly " good morning," and she and her little brother went away with him.

" Well, I never was so surprised. I had n't the least notion who they were. Who could have thought they were the little Buckhursts? They live at Buckhurst Park; I 've often heard of it, and that it 's even a finer place than pa's. At least, that it 's older, and has grander trees; but ours is very beautiful, and you can come and see me there whenever you like."

"Thank you! When do you think the hood and cloak will be ready? Because I can bring my doll and try them on at once."

Miss Botterby turned to her maid, and asked her how long she thought they would take making.

"There'll be the wheedling your ma to give you the materials, miss, and then there'll be the getting 'em bought, and then the cutting 'em out, and then the making on 'em up; so that it'll take a good bit o' time."

"About four days, do you think, Ledwick?"

"Lauk, miss! Not afore a week, at least, I should say."

"Well, then, this day week I shall expect you," said Miss Botterby, shaking hands with me and walking away with her maid, while Peep and I took our way downhill.

"You'll allow that she's rude now, Bab, I suppose. You saw how she behaved to those other children, till she found out who they were; and to us she's little better. Not that I want her to shake hands, I'm sure, but she is n't civil enough to shake hands with me or say 'good morning' to me. Not that I care, though."

"But you 're not very civil to her, Peep. That was why she asked me to go to Botterby House, and not you, I dare say."

"I don't want to go there, and I should n't go there if she asked me ever so much. She 's a rude, vulgar girl, though she is so rich. Now, the other little girl is very different; for all her coarse straw hat and her stuff frock, you can see at once she 's a little lady. I knew the moment I saw her that she was not a poor common child."

"She said she *is* poor, — at least, not rich."

"Ah, I suppose not rich for a girl who has a father and mother with 'Sir James and Lady' before their names."

While Peep and I were still talking of the children we had met, we reached the village and were passing the cottage where Miss King had lodged. I stopped for a moment, looking at it and thinking of her and wondering whether she was Uncle's wife by this time, when from out of the door ran a young woman, who came up to me, and said, —

" Please, miss, ain't you Captain Bruff's little girl? Missus thinks you are, and bids me ask if you 'd just step in a moment, as she 's got something to tell you."

## CHAPTER XI.

FOLLOWED the young woman —
who I guessed must be Mrs. Hodg-
kin's servant, that Sue had told me
was called Bet — into the cottage,
where I found Mrs. Hodgkin waiting for me
in the parlor.

"My dear young miss," said she, "I made
bold to have you called in here, because I
wanted to tell you something and to show
you something. I had a great respect for
Mrs. King, — she was quite the gentlewoman;
and her sweet good daughter, too, — there's
few like her for dutifulness and right-doing,
and always such a pretty polite way with her
to everybody, the lowest as well as the highest, — and I felt more for them in their sor-
rows than I can say. When Miss King was
working her fingers to the bone, and wearing

herself to a thread to earn their living, it
was bad enough; but when the mother was
taken ill, and the daughter got as pale as a
ghost, sitting up night after night nursing her,
yet stitching hard all day just the same, my
heart fairly bled for them. The evening before Mrs. King took to her bed, never to rise
from it,—more's the pity!—she had in her
hands this."

Mrs. Hodgkin pulled open a table-drawer
and took from it a half-finished stocking with
four knitting-needles sticking in it, and the
point of one of them into a ball of cotton as
well.

"Mrs. King used to knit all her own and
her daughter's stockings, and she sighed when
she put this down; and I heard her say softly
to herself, for I chanced to be close to her
arm-chair while she said it, and her daughter
happened to be at a little distance, ' Who
knows whether I shall ever finish it for her?
But God's will be done!' Her daughter
helped her upstairs, and I took the knitting
and needles and ball, just as they were, and

put them carefully away in this very drawer
ready for her when she next came down ; but
she never did come down, poor lady ! and the
things went out of my mind till this very
morning, when I happened to open the
drawer, after Miss King went away to be
married to your Uncle, my dear young miss,
and I thought I would give them to you to
give them to her when she comes back from
her wedding-tour. I think they'll perhaps
come better to her from you than from me ;
because she's accustomed to see me with her
mother, and it might make her cry if I gave
them to her. Whereas, if they came to her
from an innocent child, it would touch her
softly instead of sorrowfully. She'll be
glad to have them, I know, though at first
they'll make her sad. It's natural, both the
gladness and the sadness ; but the gladness
will be most, in the end, so I send them to
her. Please give them to her at some quiet
moment, my dear, with my best respects, and
tell Miss King — Mrs. Bruff, I should say —
how they were found by me. There's a look

in your young face that shows me you are just the child to tell it all to her in the right way and at the right time. Good-by, dear; I must n't keep you here any longer."

"Good-by, Mrs. Hodgkin; and thank you for giving me these to give back to her."

Peep, who had been rather impatient while Mrs. Hodgkin was talking, gave me his hand quickly, and we left the cottage. Directly we were outside, he said, —

"What long speeches Mrs. Hodgkin makes! What a time she kept us! And I 'm so hungry, and it 's long after lunch-time, I 'm certain. I wonder what Sue has got us for lunch, — a mince-pie, perhaps."

"Do you know, Peep, I think if it 's so very late, we 'd perhaps better not have lunch at all; it 'll only spoil our appetite for dinner."

"Don't you be afraid of that, Bab. I always make a good dinner, however late we have lunch."

"I 'm not quite sure that we 're not eating more than is good for us, Peep, since Uncle 's away."

"What do you mean? How can we possibly eat too much? I've often heard people say a hearty appetite is a sign of good health, and we want to be healthy, don't we?"

"Of course we do; but perhaps too many good things at once — too much mince-pie and plum-pudding at a time — may n't be quite right for us."

I said "us," because I thought Peep might n't like to have me say "you"; though it was really of him I had been thinking when I talked of eating too much and too many good things at once. Lately, since we had been only ourselves at table, he had helped himself to such large platefuls of everything, and had put such large mouthfuls into his mouth, and had swallowed them down so fast, that I was afraid he would be sick, and I did n't want him to be ill again; and besides, I did n't wish him to grow up a greedy boy, or to feel ashamed of him in any way, which I should have been if he were greedy or ill-mannered.

"As for 'quite right,' I don't know; but it's quite pleasant, and that's enough for me."

"No, Peep; 'quite pleasant' ought n't to be enough, if it 's not ' quite right' too. Remember what father used to say: ' Always do what 's right, if you want to keep happy, and to keep being a gentleman.' "

" Yes, that 's true ; and he taught me to try and keep being a gentleman, though we were so very, very poor. He said he never gave up trying to keep being a gentleman himself, and he hoped his little son would do the same all his life. It 's odd, Bab, how well I can remember many things that father used to say to me, though I was such a very wee child when he said them. He used to set me on his knee, and spoke in such a serious way and in such a grave tone, that it made me notice his words and think of them afterwards. I hope I shall never forget them. I should n't like to forget them. Do you think I shall, Bab ? "

" Not if you try to remember them, Peep. I often remind myself to think back of what father and mother said to us, and I find I can keep on remembering very well."

"I mean to try, and I'll often remind my-self to try; and then I think I shall remember, and never forget."

That day, when we reached home, Peep, of his own accord, told Sue he did n't want any lunch; so we both waited till dinner-time, and ate with excellent appetites.

Sometimes, after that, I caught Peep's eye just as he was going to help himself to another slice of bread and jam, or a second plate-ful of anything he particularly liked, and then he would stop with a laugh, and content him-self with what he had already had. I used then to laugh too; and we fell into many a piece of fun together in this way.

When a week had passed, I thought I would ask my way to Botterby House, and take my doll to have her new hood and cloak tried on; so I asked Peep if he would go with me.

"No!" he said shortly. "I told you I did n't want to go there, and I mean what I say."

"But I sha'n't like to walk there by my-self, Peep. I should be rather afraid to go alone so far; and besides, I should feel very

shy to be among strangers; for I don't know
Mrs. Botterby, though I do her daughter."

" Very little you know of either; and that
little, very disagreeable."

" I don't find her so disagreeable as you do,
Peep. It's of Mrs. Botterby I feel shy."

" Then don't go."

" But I should like to go, if you would go
with me. Do, Peep; it'll be a nice long
walk, and you'll enjoy yourself when once
you're out. And then you'll like to see the
handsome house and the beautiful old trees.
Oh, should n't you like to see those, Peep ? "

" Yes, *those;* but I don't care to see any
more of her, — that rude girl."

" You won't see much of her; you need n't
talk to her at all if you don't wish; I shall
talk to her; she and I will have so much to
say to each other about our dolls that you
need n't say a word, if you don't like to
speak. Do go with me, there's a good
Peep."

" What a coaxer you are, Bab ! "    And he
went.

The day was brilliant, and our road lay through lanes with hedgerows and skirting meadows, into which we occasionally dived, when we came to a stile or a gate, and gathered all the wild flowers we could find, which were not as many as we could have wished, since it was still winter-time. But we found some beautiful snow-drops, which made a lovely nosegay, and which Peep carried for me, as I had my doll in my arms, and she was rather heavy, being so big.

We easily found our way, by asking, as we went along, for Botterby House; and when we reached there we saw tall iron gates, with a winding road that went round a large grass-plot, in the middle of which were some beds of different colored leaves, planted in squares and three-cornered shapes, that I thought looked very bright, as there were no flowers in blossom then.

"What frightful straight patches!" said Peep. " Where are the fine old trees she talked of?"

"There are some, perhaps, at the back of the house."

We came to a broad flight of steps that looked very, very white against the bright orange-colored gravel-paths on each side, which led round the house under the windows, and at the top of the white steps there was a broad, high doorway between two large glass and gold lamps that glittered in the sun.

We went up the steps and looked about for the bell, but it was so high up that I could hardly reach it on tiptoe. However, I did manage to ring it, and the door was opened by a man in an odd coat of reddy-brown color, with worsted fringes, and cords, and dangling ends that had tips of brass to them, and yellowy-speckled bordered edges all round it. He did n't look old, though he had white hair that seemed floury all over.

He looked down at us, — for he was very tall, — and he said, —

" What might you be a-wanting, young people ? "

" We want to see Miss Botterby; she asked us to come and see her, and we 're come."

" Oh, that 's it, is it ?  Step into the hall,

and I'll go and inquire whether she'll see you."

"Of course she will ; she said so."

The tall man with the funny coat and the floury hair went away, and we had time to look about us and notice the big hall we were in, that had all sorts of odd things stuck about the walls and in the corners, — principally china; plates and flat bowls and dishes against the walls, large covered jars in the corners, — so that it looked almost like a china-shop. Presently the tall man came back, and said, —

"Miss Botterby will be glad to see you; please step this way."

He led us into a side-parlor that had a broad, high window reaching from the top of the room to the ground, and which gave a view into the garden at the back of the house. There was another grass-plot, with more beds that had square and three-cornered patches of colored leaves in them ; but round the grass-plot, and reaching far back, were some bushes and some tall trees. On a

11

sofa, near the window-curtains, which were of thick striped yellow and scarlet silk, lay a lady, with a fur coverlet over her knees, and some crochet-work in her hands. She looked lazily up at us, yawning as she looked, but rather noticingly too; while almost at the same instant in came Miss Botterby and walked towards us, holding out her hand to me.

"Ma, this is the little girl I told you about, the niece of Captain Bruff, you know; and this is her brother."

"How d' ye do?" said the lady, with another half yawn.

"I 've brought you a little nosegay," I said, as I took the bunch of snow-drops from Peep's hand and gave them to Miss Botterby. "We found them and gathered them as we came along. We were so glad to find even these few."

"Field-flowers! Weeds! Do you care for such things, Almeria?" said Mrs. Botterby to her daughter. "You had better take your young acquaintances into the conservatory, and show them our exotics; *they* are something like flowers! But stay; there's the lunch-bell. We'll have some lunch first, and then you can take them round and show them our place."

She got off her sofa, put down her crochet, took up a small dog with a blue ribbon round its neck, that had lain curled up beside her under the fur coverlet, and led the way into the dining-room, which was on the other side of the big hall.

I thought it rather nasty to see Mrs. Botterby put bits of chicken into the small dog's mouth, and then pinch off morsels of the bread beside her and put them into her own mouth with the same hand that had touched his slaver; but I tried not to think of it as I ate some of the many nice things on the lunch-table, and felt glad that they were handed round by the young man with the odd coat and the floury head instead of being helped by her.

I was also very glad to see that Peep did not take too much of the delicious jellies and creams and cakes that were at this grand lunch; but he helped himself neatly and moderately to some of them when they were handed to him.

I saw that Mrs. Botterby noticed how well he behaved and what nice manners he had, though he was such a little fellow, and I felt very proud of him and pleased with him.

After lunch Mrs. Botterby said, —

"Now, Almeria, you can take them round the grounds; but if you go beyond the conservatory, mind you put a shawl over your head and shoulders, for fear you should take cold. Oh, and take care to hold it over your mouth, when you pass out of the hot-houses into the open air. Oh, and be sure not to touch my white camellias; you know I want them all for next Saturday's dinner-party, and they are very scarce; any of the rest — the red, or pink, or streaked ones — you may have, if you want some to give a bouquet to your young acquaintances."

"All right, ma!"

But when Miss Botterby took us into the

big hall instead of going through the glass-
door that led into the garden, she said, —

"Let's go upstairs to my room first; I
want to show you how handsomely furnished
it is, and give you the hood and cloak for
your doll, — I see you've brought her with
you, — so we can put them on at once, and
you can carry her with us round the grounds
properly dressed for going out."

"Yes, that will be nice!"

We went up a wide staircase that led out
of the hall, and passed into a beautiful room
that looked more like a parlor than a bedroom, it was full of such a number of easy-
chairs and sofas covered with bright rich
stuffs, and large looking-glasses on the walls,
and thick curtains of the same color as the
coverings of the chairs on each side the
windows and round the bed.

"Ledwick, get the hood and cloak for Miss
Bruff's doll."

The maid, who came into the room at one
door as Miss Botterby and I entered at the
other, opened a drawer and took out, — oh,

*such* a lovely white cashmere hood and cloak, trimmed and lined with white satin! And when they were put on to my doll, they fitted her, — oh, so beautifully.

"Thank you, oh, thank you, Miss Botterby, for such a lovely present! It seems almost too beautiful for me to take!"

"Oh dear, no; I'm quite glad to give it you, I assure you."

"And thank you, too, Ledwick, for making them so cleverly."

"Quite welcome, I'm sure, miss."

"Give me a shawl, Ledwick; ma makes such a fuss about my wrapping up when I go in and out of the hot-houses, that I suppose I must have one."

"To be sure you must, miss. O' course your ma's careful about your health. What would she or your pa do if you was to get cold and be ill?"

As we went downstairs, Miss Botterby said to me, —

"Ledwick's a good creature and very fond of me, I do believe. But you need n't have thanked *her* for making the doll's things; I gave her orders to do it, and she obeyed me, of course, and that was all."

I was just going to tell Miss Botterby that I had felt I ought to thank Ledwick for the trouble she had taken *for me*, when I was interrupted by Peep's calling out to me, —

" I 've been seeing such lots of amusing things that Joe has shown me, — croquet-balls and croquet-mallets, he called them, and said they were for playing at a game called croquet."

" Joe ? "

" Yes, Bab ; I asked him his name, and he told me it was Joe."

Peep looked towards the tall young man with the odd coat and the floury head, who was standing near the glass door leading into the garden, ready to open it for us as we passed out.

# CHAPTER XII.

H E means our footman," said Miss Botterby, when we were in the garden.

"What a curious coat he has on!" I said.

"It's our livery," said she. "It's handsome, is n't it?"

"Why does he put flour on his head?"

"He wears powder; livery footmen, belonging to great people, generally do."

"Are you great people?" asked Peep.

"Of course; pa's one of the richest men in the city. But look; this is the conservatory. Is n't it handsome? Pa spared no expense in building it and having it well filled with the dearest plants and flowers."

The raptures both Peep and I fell into at the sight of these in full bloom, though it

was winter, seemed very much to please Miss
Botterby. She gathered each of us a beautiful bunch of camellias of the richest colors,
and Peep put his up to his nose to smell
them.

"They've no scent," said she.

"No, none," he answered; "I can't find
the least smell in them. I don't like them
half so much as the roses in Uncle's garden."

"But roses are common flowers, and camellias are very rare. They only grow in
greenhouses. I suppose your Uncle has n't
a greenhouse, has he?"

"No," said Peep. "But he has a garden
full, full, full of roses, that Ned Carter keeps
well attended to, and makes them blossom
quite late in the year. He's very clever
at it."

"Who's Ned Carter?"

"A very nice boy who comes and gardens
for us."

"Pa keeps four gardeners and a gardener's
boy. With all our hot-houses and large
grounds we of course want as many."

"How pure and lovely those white camellias are! No wonder Mrs. Botterby prizes them so much," I said.

"Yes, they 're beautiful, ain't they? Ma 's so fussy over them; but one won't be missed. You *shall* have one; you can hide it from her, you know, as you go out. She 'll never see it."

"Oh, no, no! Don't, pray, pray, Miss Botterby!"

But before I could prevent her, she had plucked off one of the white flowers and held it out to me.

"Don't take it, Bab!" shouted Peep, eagerly.

"No, of course not," I answered. "Thank you, very, very much, Miss Botterby, but I can't take it!"

"Why not?"

"Mrs. Botterby told you not to gather the white ones, you know; she said you might take any but those for us."

"Oh, ma fusses so ridiculously; she fusses about everything."

"She particularly said, not the white camellias. I can't, I can't take them."

"But it's gathered now; you must take it."

"I can't."

"Say you won't," said Peep.

"No, indeed, Miss Botterby, I cannot, I
will not; you yourself must see that I ought
not."

"And after all I've done to please you,
you won't oblige me by taking this stupid
camellia. Don't you see that it'll get me
into trouble with ma if she finds I've gathered it against her positive orders. What
am I to do with it? If you won't take it,
and help me to hide it from her, I shall get
into a fine scrape with her, and she'll tell pa,
and I shall get into disgrace with him too."

"I'm very, very sorry; but I really can't."

"And after my giving you such a handsome hood and cloak for your doll, too!
Fine thanks, — not to do such a little thing
to please me!"

I was so miserable to see her so vexed,
and it seemed so ungrateful in me, that I

felt half inclined to put out my hand for the
white flower she kept holding towards me.

"Don't take it, Bab!" almost screamed
Peep.

Suddenly she snatched back the camellia
and said, —

"I know what I can do!"

She began hurriedly digging up the earth
in the large pot where the plant of white
camellias grew, with a bit of stick she found
near; and, plunging the gathered flower deep
into the mould, covered it up close, and
pressed the earth smoothly on the top.

"There! nobody will ever notice anything.
I shall never be found out.  Come, let's go
and see the hot-houses."

But neither Peep nor I could so soon forget what had passed; and we followed Miss
Botterby round the wonders of the place
without really enjoying the peach-house, or
the vine-house, or the pine-house, or anything else that she showed us with her usual
question of "Is n't it handsome?" and her
usual assurance that "it cost lots of money."

We both felt very uncomfortable, for I
could see that Peep was quite as put out as
I was. One of the things that most troubled
me was, that I did n't like to keep the beautiful hood and cloak Miss Botterby had given
me, after she had reproached me with her
gift; and yet I hardly knew how I could tell
her so. But at last I got up courage to say:

"I would rather not keep these, Miss Botterby," and I began taking them off my
doll.

"What are you about? Don't, for good-
ness sake, give me back my present to you.
Ma will be sure to notice the doll has n't got
them on when you go to take leave of her;
and then all will come out, and I shall be just
as badly off as ever."

"Give 'em back, Bab!" said Peep.

"If you do, I shall have to give them to
Ledwick to take 'em out of the house without
ma seeing them; and I shall have to manage
for you to go away without taking leave of
her."

"Manage as you like!" said Peep.

I folded up the beautiful hood and cloak with trembling hands and gave them back to Miss Botterby, saying, —

" I'm very sorry, I'm *very* sorry; it was very good and kind of you to give them to me, — but I *must*."

She snatched them from me, tucked them hastily under the shawl that was muffled round her head and shoulders, and said, —

" Oh, nonsense! Sorry! sorry! Why could n't you have done what I asked you? Sorry! Yes, I dare say! "

" Indeed, indeed, I am sorry, Miss Botterby! "

But she did n't stay to listen to me; she walked straight into the house and into the room where we had first seen Mrs. Botterby.

There was no one there, and Joe came forward to his young mistress, saying, —

" If you please, miss, missus has gone upstairs to lie down for an hour, and left word she was n't to be disturbed."

" All right," said Miss Botterby, with her face suddenly clearing up.  Then turning to

Peep and me, she said, "Good-by! It's all blown over, you see; so you can come and see me another day as soon as you like, and then I'll show you how to play at croquet."

We took leave of her, walking out of the tall iron gates into the road without speaking a word to each other; but when we turned into a shady lane, Peep broke silence by saying, —

"I'm so glad you gave her back her present; I could n't have borne you to keep it."

"I should never have had any pleasure in looking at it again, or in seeing it on my dolly. I should always have been reminded of — "

"Yes; you'd always have thought of Miss Almeria Botterby as she looked while cramming that white flower under the mould. What a bad face she has! How ugly she looked while she was hiding it away! She's not only a rude girl, but a bad girl; and not only a bad girl, but an ugly girl."

"Not ugly, Peep. She has blue eyes and light hair and very pretty pink cheeks."

"I don't care what eyes and hair and cheeks she has; she's a horribly ugly girl!"

We talked on till we came to the blacksmith's forge, where we stopped for a moment to watch some horses being shod. We noticed that the old coachman we had seen before was standing by, watching also. He touched his hat when he saw us; and Peep said, —

"Good afternoon, Stubbs!"

"You know my name, young master."

"Yes, Stubbs. I heard Miss Buckhurst call you so."

"She and Master Jamie went off of their own heads, down yon lane, while I stopped here to see th' horses were rightly shod. If you're going that way, you might just give a look after young master and miss. Would you be so good? And please say the shoeing's wellnigh done, and we'd better be jogging back to Buckhurst Park. They *would* come with me to-day, though I said I had to walk th' horses here and back. But they're main fond of a long ramble wi' me, bless their little hearts! Would you be so good, sir, if you 're going that way ? "

" Certainly, Stubbs; we *are* going that way."

I rather wondered to hear Peep say this, as we had n't talked of going down the lane that turned off at the corner where Trebbitt's forge was. However, I supposed he had thought of going, as I knew he liked throwing stones into a pond that was there, and making "ducks and drakes" with them. It was a shallow pond, shelving down from the edge at one side, where horses were taken to water. It had been covered with ice lately, when a good deal of sliding and skating had taken place on it; but since the last few days there had been a thaw, and the ice was all gone.

As we drew near the spot we heard loud shrieks and cries, which made us hurry on to see what was the matter. To our great dismay we saw little Miss Buckhurst and Jamie up to their knees in the pond, and screaming wildly. We ran forward, and she called out:

12

"Oh, help us out! help us out! Jamie ventured into the water after his whip, which had dropped in and floated away; but his feet stuck in the mud and he could n't get back again. Then I waded in after him; but my feet stuck too, and I could n't move. I could only hold him by the hand, but could n't drag him out."

"Hold his hand still! Hold it fast! Be sure you don't let it go!" I cried. "Hold it tight, tight!"

I looked round, and, by good fortune, saw a large long pole of wood lying under a tree close to the pond-side, and not far from where Peep and I stood. I told him to help me to lift it up. It was heavy, but not too heavy for his and my strength put together. We raised it and pushed it into the pond as near as we could to where the two children were standing, shivering, hand in hand.

"Put out the hand you 're not holding your brother by, and try to catch hold of the pole," I said.

The little girl seemed quickly to understand

what I wanted her to do, and succeeded in clutching the end of the pole.

"Draw it to you, and tell your brother to put his other hand upon it too. That's it! Now, both of you hold by it, and it'll bear you up till we can get help. Peep, run as fast as you can back to the forge and tell Stubbs and Trebbitt what has happened, and fetch them here."

While Peep ran off, I watched the two children, and saw that the pole had reached them just in time, for they had fast been getting too frightened and too shivering to have been able to hold up much longer by themselves. I spoke cheerily to them, and they answered more and more cheerily in return; so that by the time the men came from the forge they were quite merry, and laughing at the plight they were in.

They were soon got out of the pond, and we all hurried back to the forge, that their wet clothes might be thoroughly dried at the blacksmith's roaring fire. Polly Trebbitt and her mother made themselves very useful in giving proper attention to the two dripping children, who were now in high spirits at their adventure.

"If Sir James comes to know it, though, it 'll be a bad job for me," said Stubbs, dolefully. "He 'll never let me take you out for a walk again; he 'll say I ought n't to have let you out of my sight, and so I ought n't."

"It was we who *would* go," said Jamie.

"It 's as much as my place is worth, if Sir James comes to know it, any how."

"He must know it, of course. I shall tell my father how it happened, myself, Stubbs; and you 'll see, he won't be angry with you when he knows it was all our fault."

"All your fault, Miss Mabel? No, no, it was mine! I ought to ha' known better than to let two such little things as you stray off alone."

"Leave it to me, Stubbs. I shall tell my father the truth, the exact truth; and you 'll see he won't be angry. He never is, when we tell him the whole truth. And he won't be angry now, when Jamie and I are both safe

and sound, as we are ; because of your help
just in time," said Mabel, turning to Peep and
me.

"Thank you both ! Oh, thank you !"

"We were very glad to be there to help
you."

"Very, very glad," said Peep, earnestly.

"I do think you saved our lives. Thank
you, dear, again and again, for your good
thought of the pole. You'll let me call you
'dear,' won't you?" she said to me.

"Oh, yes, yes; and thank you for liking to
call me so."

We all four took leave of each other very
happily and affectionately ; and as Peep and
I walked home together, he said to me, —

"Did you see how sweet her eyes looked,
and how they sparkled when she thanked us?
How pretty she is ! how very, very pretty !"

"She looks more sweet than pretty, I
think."

"Oh, both, both ! She's as sweet as she's
pretty, and as pretty as she's sweet. She
has the very darlingest face I ever saw. It's

even darlinger than yours, Bab; and yet,
yours is the dearest in the world to me.    I
have always felt I had rather look at it than
at any other; but now I would like often to
look at hers too.    Do you think we shall
often see her again ?    I could n't bear to think
we should not see her sometimes again."

"I don't believe we shall see very much of
her, Peep.    You know her father and mother
are Sir James and Lady Buckhurst, and they
may be rather ' high and proud,' and not care
for us to be very much friends with their
children."

"I don't think Mabel's father and mother
can be ' high and proud;' she looks so gentle
and meek and sweet herself.    Do you think
she would like you to call her ' Mabel'?" said
Peep.

"I'm afraid she 'd think it too — too —"

"Too intimate ?    She asked you to let her
call you ' dear,' you know."

"Yes, she did; but, if you notice, I did n't
ask her in return to let me call her ' dear.'
I thought she might n't like it; and yet that

she would n't like to tell me so, for fear I might be hurt by what she said."

" I can't be sure, of course; but I feel somehow certain she would n't mind being called ' dear,' by you, Bab."

" Perhaps so; and if she did n't mind it, I should like very much to call her ' dear,' for she is — very dear."

" Very, very dear ! " said Peep.

Next morning the postman brought a letter to the door.  Sue took it in, and brought it to me.

"It 's for Uncle, I suppose.  I 'll put it with the rest of his letters, that have come since he 's been away."

" I think it 's for you, miss."

" For me, Sue ? "

" Yes, miss ; look at it."

It was directed in large letters — letters so big and so clear that I could read them quite easily ; and I saw " For Bab and Peep " written upon it, with " Trafalgar Lodge " underneath.  It was the first letter we had ever received, so we were both in great delight.

Inside, the writing was very big and clear also; therefore I could make out every word, and I read the letter straight through to Peep:

DEAR CHILDREN, — Your Uncle and I hope to be with you two days after this letter reaches you, as I am now getting quite well and strong again. The sea has done us both great good, and we have enjoyed being out all day on the beach and letting the wind blow upon our cheeks. Some day we hope to bring you two with us here, and show you the sea and the beach, where you can pick up shells, and where Peep can fill his wheelbarrow with sand and beautiful sea-weeds. I will not write any more, because I hope to tell you all myself when I come home. So good-by till then. I am

Your affectionate aunt,

PENELOPE BRUFF.

P. S. — Uncle sends his love to you both, and so do I.

"She knows about my wheelbarrow! She *must* be a nice woman, to care when Uncle told her I had one. I suppose she asked whether it was big enough to hold sand and sea-weed. What a heap I will pile up in it!"

I told Sue the good news that Uncle and his wife were soon coming home; and she helped me to arrange the rooms with holly and evergreens, to make the house look pretty and seem to welcome them with brightness.

"It's fit a bride should find her new home at its very neatest and nicest," said Sue, "and we'll make it so all we can, won't we? It shall be in apple-pie order, I warrant!"

When everything was burnished to its utmost everywhere, I went into the room that was meant for their own, and on the white frilled muslin covering that Sue had put over the toilet-table, I placed the half-knitted stocking, needles, and ball of cotton, — just as they had been given to me, — in the midst of a wreath of ivy with its dark purple berries and shining green leaves, which I had made myself.

## CHAPTER XIII.

N the day Uncle and our new aunt were expected home, it was all that Peep and I could do to keep still. We were perpetually running out into the garden and down to the gate, that we might hear the very first sound of wheels; for we knew that they would come in a coach, on account of the trunks and bandboxes they had to bring from the seaside where they had been staying. At last, just as we had almost given up listening and looking out, and were sitting down to have some lunch that Sue had persuaded us to eat, lest we should be too hungry if we waited any longer for them, there came a distant rumble along the road, a sudden stop at the gate, and out we both darted to meet them. Not only Uncle, but his wife, gave us

many hearty kisses and hugs, and we all went trooping into the house together, a merry, laughing, joyful party.

" I 'm glad to see something on the table ready to eat," said Uncle, rubbing his hands, " for our journey has made us as hungry as hunters. Come, Mrs. Bruff, my dear, take your place at the head of the table at once, and do the honors for us."

She sat down quietly, easily, just as if she had been accustomed to sit there always, and smiled round upon us all so pleasantly that we did not feel the least strange or uncomfortable at finding some one new among our family party. I had never seen Uncle look so bright; or so alive to what was passing round him, before ; he never fell into silences, or seemed unnoticing, once while the meal was going on ; and when it was over, instead of turning round his chair and staring into the fire, he looked at his wife and asked her if she were tired, and whether she would n't go upstairs and take her bonnet off, and take a rest.

"Little Bab, here, shall go with you and show you your room. You don't know what a capital little manager she is, though she is such a mite."

"Yes, I think I do; I have seen before now how capitally she manages when she has only herself to rely upon, and is nursing some one she is fond of. We know something of each other already, Bab; don't we?"

She put her arm round me as she spoke and drew me close to her, keeping me so even while we went up the stairs together, chatting quietly to me all the time.

"I was some comfort to you, my child, when you were in trouble about your little brother; and now, Bab, you do not know, you cannot know, the great, great comfort you are to me."

"I, Miss Ki — I mean Mrs —"

"Aunty, — Aunty Pen! Call me so always now, my dear."

"Yes, Aunty; but I don't know how I can be a comfort to you. I? I?"

"I told you you could not know, Bab.

How should you understand what an immense comfort your young artless ways, your pretty childish liking for me, your mere little genuine self here, is to me on my coming home first to my new life? No; you do not know, — you cannot know!"

She spoke this as if more to herself than to me, though she fixed her eyes on mine, looking down at me as we went up the stairs together, so that I can quite well remember the exact words she said.

"Well, I think I do begin to know a little what you mean, Miss — Aunty. I can fancy that somebody — even such a very young somebody as I am — must be a sort of comfort to you to find already in the house where you come to live for the first time and for all the rest of your life. Yes, I think I do begin to understand. It makes you feel not quite so much a stranger as you might have done if Peep and I were not here, — Peep and I that you helped in our trouble, you know."

By the time I had said this, we had entered the room which was to be her own, and

I saw her eyes at once fasten upon the unfinished knitting that lay on the white muslin toilet-cover in the midst of the wreath of green leaves.

"You guess what it is?" I whispered. "Mrs. Hodgkin gave it to me to give to you; she kept it safely for you, and sent it you through me."

I saw her turn very pale, and her eyes filled with tears; but she said in a quiet, low voice, —

"Yes, that evening; I recollect it was left when — yes, I recollect. I like it to come to me through you, my little Bab, my tender-hearted little Bab, who knows, like me, what it is to have lost a mother, a dear, dear mother; don't you, darling?"

I nodded gently, kissed her as she sat down near the toilet-table, and then crept out of the room as softly as I could.

I found Uncle and Peep at high romps when I went down into the parlor, — Uncle chasing Peep round the room, scampering and laughing with him in a way that I had never seen before, as if he enjoyed the fun himself, instead of hardly ever noticing either of us. I joined in the game, so that when Aunt Pen came downstairs she was amused to see the bustle and hear the uproar that was going on. Her face was smiling and calm, but it looked still rather white. Uncle observed this directly, and said, —

" I 'm afraid the journey has fatigued you, my Penn'orth; you must n't overdo it, you know; you 're not quite strong yet. Remember it 's a bargain; you promised me to rest whenever you felt tired."

" Yes, I remember. I 'm going to rest by sitting in this nice easy-chair and telling the children a story, if they would like to hear one."

" Oh, a story! a story!" exclaimed both Peep and I. " We do love to hear a story!"

" We 'll all listen," said Uncle, as he drew a chair beside his wife, while Peep and I settled ourselves on the rug at her feet.

" Why do you call her 'Penn'orth,' Uncle?" said Peep, suddenly. "I thought her name was Penelope. It used to be Miss Penelope King; and now, I suppose it's Mrs. Penelope Bruff."

"Well, so it is, my boy; but Pen's short for Penelope, and I make it into Penn'orth, because she's a good pennyworth to me."

We all laughed heartily at Uncle's way of saying this, till Peep broke in with, —

"Hush! Don't let's laugh any more and lose time. Let's have the story."

"What kind of a story shall it be? What is it to be about?"

"About lions and tigers," said Peep. "Or, no, — stay; let it be about kings and queens and genies and Sinbads and Aladdins and forty thieves and wicked enchanters, — such as father used to tell us when he took us on his knee."

"An Eastern story? Well, then, once upon a time — "

"What's the name of the story, Aunt Pen?"

"'The story of Prince Zaraf and his Mother,' and it begins: Once upon a time there was a king called Gordubar, who had a wife called Azuralma and a little son called Prince Zaraf. This king was a proud, imperious man, who could n't bear to be contradicted in anything he said or did or ordered."

" What's ' imperious' ? " said Peep.

" Oh, Peep, don't interrupt! " I said.

" ' Imperious' means commanding, domineering, too fond of having his own way. Unfortunately, Prince Zaraf took more after his father than his mother, who was gentle and very forbearing. The little prince would throw himself into violent rages if he were thwarted in the slightest thing he wished, and he liked to have his own way, right or wrong. He would even burst into fits of passion and resist his own father, if King Gordubar would not let him have something he wanted, and would storm and rave and stamp about the room like a little fury. This brought father and son into many an unseemly anger against each other, which the good, gentle queen tried in vain to appease; but while Prince Zaraf was still very young, he had a severe lesson

13

which for a time made him try to keep
watch over his temper lest it should have the
fatal effect, in his own case, which to his dismay he beheld it have in his father's.

"It chanced that Gordubar's vizier, or
prime minister, was a very sage, prudent, benevolent man, who had deeply at heart the
welfare of his royal master's subjects, and for
whose sake he would venture even to oppose
the will of the king himself, when it decided
upon any measure which the minister thought
was contrary to the interests of the people.
Once it so happened that King Gordubar gave
an order to his army which appeared to the
vizier, Verasmin, so extremely unjust and in-
jurious toward the peaceful citizens and peas-
ants of the kingdom that he boldly repre-
sented to the monarch the mischief that would
follow if his order were carried out, and be-
sought him to reconsider his commands. Enraged to be thus opposed, Gordubar roughly
bade his wise counsellor immediately see that
the royal order was fulfilled, and take heed
how he hesitated or disobeyed. Verasmin

replied firmly that he owed obedience to his
sovereign, but that he owed a duty also to the
people, whom he would not see tyrannically
treated without at least trying to persuade the
king to reverse his decree. From roughness
and contempt Gordubar proceeded to insolence
and insult, overwhelming his good minister
with foul words and threats, until, in the very
midst of his storm of wrath, the king suddenly fell back, stone dead, having broken a
blood-vessel by his intemperate rage. Queen
Azuralma hoped that out of this terrible
calamity might come useful warning to her
young son; that he might learn to curb his
own disposition ere the time came when he
should have to reign in his father's stead;
and meantime, by her own gentle wisdom,
aided by the sage experience and prudence
of Verasmin, she governed the kingdom as
regent. For a while, the example of his
father's fate acted well upon Prince Zaraf;
but after a time he fell into his old habit
of going into furious fits of anger whenever
he was contradicted or disappointed. Once

when he was giving way to one of these vehement outbreaks his mother unexpectedly came into the apartment where he was. She went straight up to where he stood fuming and raging, and laying her hand softly upon his arm, she said, —

" ' Alas! my son, I see that even the direful scene you once beheld has ceased to have controlling effect. But if that fail to move you to self-correction, let what I am now going to tell you have force to cure you of your malady of temper. Know, that should you ever suffer yourself to give way to such fatal excess of anger as shall cause me equally fatal excess of grief, it will cast me into the power of a great enchanter, who will carry me away beyond your reach. I shall fall into his power, and it will be you, my own son, my dearest Zaraf, who will have brought this misery of separation upon us both.'

" The prince, shocked and sobered, promised his mother, with tears of repentance, to try to obtain better control of his passionate disposition; and for a long period he suc-

ceeded in gaining some mastery over it.    The
years passed by, and the boy grew into the
youth, and the youth into the young man;
when, just as he attained the age to reign, his
sage minister, the Vizier Verasmin, died, leaving the young prince to mount the throne
with none to guide and assist him save the
queen-mother, Azuralma.    Her gentle advice,
her lenient counsels, were of great avail, and
King Zaraf governed well and justly, and
became popular with his subjects.

"On one occasion, however, a Numidian
slave of his, whom he had trusted with some
grave charge, misunderstood his orders and
caused a favorite plan of King Zaraf's to fail.
In a frenzy of wrath to see his views frus-
trated, he commanded the slave to be forth-
with strangled; and though the wretched
man pleaded mistake, not wilful disobedience
or guilt, Zaraf persisted in his command.
Azuralma, hearing of this stern sentence, has-
tened to her son's presence and entreated
him to withdraw it, pleading hard to have the
miserable slave's life spared, and seeking to

move her son to mercy by telling him that
this slave had long been a faithful and devoted
servitor.  But Zaraf was in too great a tu-
mult of foiled will and enraged resentment
to listen even to her, and he turned angrily
away to enforce immediate execution of his
command.  At that moment a thick gray
mist filled the whole of the presence-chamber
where the court were assembled, and where
Zaraf was giving way to his cruel and ungovernable fury.  Appalled by the sudden veil-
ing of the light, he looked round and dimly
saw a gigantic figure extend its hand over
Queen Azuralma's head, who, casting sad,
despairing looks at her son to the last, was
wafted away from his sight.  Zaraf fell to the
ground in a deadly swoon, from which he was
with difficulty recovered by his attendants;
but as soon as his senses were restored, he
sent out guards in every direction to seek his
mother, and endeavor to discover what had
become of her and whither she had been con-
veyed.  No trace of her, however, could be
found; and it was whispered that those who

went in search of her never returned, but were carried away also. A mystery, a dread uncertainty as to the disappearance of the queen-mother and of those who were sent in pursuit of her, seemed to prevail among the general court; and as for King Zaraf, he was completely overwhelmed by his loss, and stricken down by sorrow. He remained secluded in his own chamber, prostrate body and mind; for his deep dejection brought on sickness, and he was really ill and unable to move."

"My dear Penn'orth, you will have to break off your story," said Uncle, "for here's Sue come to lay the cloth for dinner, and I won't have you overtire yourself by talking too much at a time."

"I hope Aunt Pen won't be too tired to begin again after dinner," said Peep. "I do so want to hear the rest of the story."

"We must see how she feels; she's had a long journey to-day, you know, Peep."

"Ay, ay, my little Bab, well said! We'll see about it, won't we? We'll not let her do too much, will we?" said Uncle.

## CHAPTER XIV

FTER dinner, when Aunt Pen was comfortably arranged again by the fire, and we had all taken our places round her, she went on with her story.

"For a long time the young King Zaraf lay in this state of misery and restless pain; for he could not rest, though he was unable to get up and move about. He tossed to and fro, racked by the memory that it was his own rash ungovernable temper which had caused his fondly loved mother to be torn from him.

"'She warned me! She told me what would be the consequence! She warned me! She warned me!'

"This was one of the thoughts that perpetually stung him with remorse. Another was, —

" ' Where is she ? Whither has she been spirited away ? Where, where is she ? Oh, where, *where* is she ? '

" Then he would fling himself round in tortured, baffled longing and fruitless desire to again behold her.

" At length, after a weary night of such impatient repinings, towards morning he fell into a quieter slumber than any he had enjoyed of late, from which he awoke in a softened mood, and with a strange feeling of peace and submission. He looked languidly round his sick-room; the watch-lights were burning low, the attendants had fallen asleep, the half-darkness of the apartment was broken by a slanting ray of pale light that came from between the heavy folds of a rich curtain drawn before the window, showing him that the dawn was at hand. An unconquerable wish to go and seek his mother himself at once came upon him, and he rose from his bed, threw on some wrapping garment that lay near, and went quietly towards a communicating passage that led up from his own

apartments into those which his mother had
formerly occupied. On entering the chamber
where he had so often stood beside her knee
and told her his childish troubles when a boy,
and where he had so often received her ca-
resses and comforting words, her soothing
advice, her gentle and wise admonitions, Zaraf
melted into tears, and stood for some moments
wrapped in tender recollections. Suddenly
his attention was attracted towards a small
door, not far from the bed's head, — a door
which he had never observed there before.
He went towards it, opened it, and perceived,
by the dim light that pervaded the room and
even penetrated within this small door, that
there was a narrow winding staircase leading
upward, he knew not whither. He ascended
the steps, and, on reaching their summit, found
himself in a long gallery, with a range of windows on one side that looked out upon a fine
expanse of scenery which surrounded the
palace. The dawning light was gaining,
gaining, and the whole landscape was suf-
fused with a soft roseate hue blended with

the pale blue of the sky, amid which the fast-disappearing stars and the slender silver bow of a waning moon were just faintly visible. He looked forth on the fair view, and his heart softened more and more.

"'Oh, if I could but find her, — could but know, at least, where she is!'

"He sighed deeply as he murmured these words under his breath, and turned from the window to pursue his way along the gallery, at the farther end of which he perceived another door. On passing through this he came to corridor after corridor, leading through a succession of side rooms that seemed deserted and dismantled, and through diverging smaller passages with apparently more disused rooms on either side, — a perplexing labyrinth of places he had never seen in this out-of-the-way uppermost story of his own palace. At last he came to another long gallery, at the termination of which he saw a golden door, stately, superb, and magnificently wide. He went eagerly towards it, yet with a certain feeling of

awe and trembling expectation. The door
yielded to his hand, and he entered. He
beheld a spacious chamber, lofty, vast, and
hung round with azure and fleecy folds of
pure white."

"What's azure?" whispered Peep.

"Oh, Peep, *don't* interrupt! 'Azure' means
blue," I said.

"Across the centre of this chamber there
was a strong grating of iron bars," continued
Aunt Pen; "and behind this grating Zaraf
saw his dear mother, with her sad, gentle eyes
bent upon him, as he sprang forward with a
fond exclamation of joy to try and clasp her
in his arms. But the strong iron bars were
there; and beside her stood a grim figure,
gigantic, all-powerful, with outstretched arm
that seemed to hold her spellbound,—a figure
in dusky robes, with dry bones and a cruel
face. Making one wild dash against the bars,
and finding he could not force his way through
them, Zaraf rushed out of the chamber to get
help, shouting for his guards and attendants
to come and beat down the iron grating.

As he flew back along the gallery, he heard the golden door close behind him with a deep clanging noise, and when his guards came in answer to the young king's cries there was no golden door to be seen. In vain he sought, in vain every effort was made to discover this door, in vain search was diligently pursued along each corridor and passage that Zaraf thought he had passed through. Even he himself could not retrace his way with any certainty, and even to him they appeared unlike what they were when he had first traversed them. Distracted, bewildered, he wandered to and fro, endeavoring to lead his followers, but failing utterly in his attempt.

"He sank again into a state of morbid inaction and despondency. He neglected State affairs, and left his kingdom to be ruled as best it might. Fortunately, to Verasmin had succeeded as vizier a son scarcely less well qualified than the father; so that, notwithstanding the young monarch's neglect, the public welfare was still cared for.

" An interval elapsed, when in the dead of
the night, in profound darkness, Zaraf felt
himself irresistibly impelled to creep up to
his mother's old apartments and kneel beside
the bed where she had lain. He groped his
way softly up the communicating passage,
and knelt down in an humble, childlike, trust-
ing way. He had often come to this room in
daylight, but never could he find the small
door near the bed. Now, when he raised his
head, after his devout humility of supplica-
tion, he saw a ray of moonlight pierce the
darkness and shed its silvery beam on the
very door he sought. He rose with beating
heart and went towards it, passing readily
through, up the narrow winding staircase,
and finding himself once more in the long
gallery with the range of windows on one
side, from which he now gazed upon a scene
of exquisite splendor, — the whole landscape
bathed in the soft yet brilliant moonshine.
But he hurried on, and to his inexpressible
delight he found himself again threading the
same maze of corridors, passages, and side

rooms as before, until he reached the uppermost gallery, where at its farther end he saw — oh, joy ! — the stately golden door. Again it yielded to his hand, and again on entering he beheld the azure chamber, with its fleecy hangings of pure white, its grating of iron bars, behind which still was there his dear mother, while beside her stood the dusky-robed, grim, giant figure with its outstretched bony arm and cruel face. The young king cast himself on the ground, mutely, with clasped hands, and with beseeching eyes fastened upon hers, which regarded him with tender, undying affection.

"'Zaraf, my son, it is permitted me to speak to you; be contented with thus much of comfort. So long as you are in softened mood, so long as you are patient, submissive, trying to perfect your imperfect nature and raise it into better and worthier condition, so long will you be permitted to find your way to the golden door, to enter the azure chamber, to hold converse with your mother who loves you, who watches over you with no less fondness than of old. Farewell for the present, and remember!'

"As she uttered the last words, her form and that of the grim figure seemed to fade from before the eyes of Zaraf, the azure chamber became indistinct and unsolid, and he sank down senseless. Many times after this the young king quietly sought and found the golden door, holding in the azure chamber much converse with his mother, whose gentle advice and wise counsels aided him to govern well and nobly. He grew thoughtful for his people, benevolent towards them, and greatly patient with their errors. It befell that a great pestilence visited his kingdom, and Zaraf not only took measures to prevent as much as possible the extension of the evil, but he gave personal inspection and tendance to the sufferers. This ended in his taking the malady himself, and he lay in his own room sick almost unto death. The chief suffering of which he was conscious was an aching desire to have strength enough for dragging himself up to his mother in the azure chamber; but his weary, fever-worn limbs forbade the hope each time he made an attempt to leave his bed; and at length he gave up even this idea, and quietly surrendered himself to mere passive lying there, thinking tenderly, gratefully, placidly of her who had been his guardian angel through life, and now became his sole happiness of thought. The heat and glare of the noonday sun had been screened from the apartment by cool green outer shutters and rich thick curtains within; but suddenly Zaraf became aware of a bland glory of light that spread around him, and as he turned his eyes towards its centre, he beheld, at a few paces from his bedside, the golden door in all its stately magnificence. He mustered what slight remaining strength he had, and threw himself from his couch in a transport of joy, finding the golden portal yield like lightest down to his touch. There, within, was the azure chamber, the fleecy purity of cloudlike hangings, the grating of iron bars, and the gentle mother with her eyes of love, now radiantly happy, and her face beaming with an ecstasy

14

of welcome. The giant figure was also there; but the dusky robes looked mere soft, gray, shadowy folds of drapery, and the face, no longer cruel, wore a less frightful aspect. Zaraf staggered forward, faltering out, —

"' Mother, beloved mother! Not so much do I now desire to have thee back, as to come myself to thee!'

"The bars melted before him, he reached his mother's breast, and they were folded in each other's embrace nevermore to part."

Aunt Pen paused, and we were all for some moments silent. Then Peep drew a long breath, and said, —

"I 'm glad!"

"Glad Zaraf and his mother are together again at last, or glad the story has come to an end, my boy?"

"Oh, Uncle, you know which! You know I 'm glad Zaraf grew good and found his mother forever. I like stories to end happily, and this story does."

"Yes," I said.

"Yes, it ends happily," said both Uncle

and Aunt Pen, softly. "And now I think our young folk ought to be travelling towards Bedfordshire, ought n't they?" said Uncle in a cheery tone, after he and Aunty had been looking into the fire for a little while.

Whereupon Peep and I gave both of them a hug and a kiss and a "good night," and thanking Aunt Pen for her story, we went off to bed.

Next morning we had a bright, merry breakfast; and after Uncle had gone away to town, Aunt Pen showed us some pretty picture-books that he and she had brought from the seaside for us. She first told us about the pictures in them, and then asked us if we could read the nice large print of the stories in the books. Peep hung his head, then looked up briskly, and said, —

"Bab can!"

"Only a very little. I can only read when the letters are very big."

"Would you like to be able to read big letters, like Bab, Peep? And would you, Bab, like to read small letters as well as big ones?"

"That I should!" both of us said at once.

"Then I will teach you, dears. We'll have nice little reading-lessons every morning as soon as Uncle goes away to town after breakfast, so that we shall be able to surprise him some day with the pleasure of hearing you each read a story to him out of the books he has brought you."

"Oh, that will be nice! Would you begin to teach us at once, Aunt Pen? To-day, — this very morning?"

"Yes, Bab; and I'll begin with Peep. So you can take your doll's work, and make her a new pinafore while I show him his letters."

"I'm afraid I should n't know how to cut out a pinafore, Aunt Pen."

"Then I'll cut out one for you, and you shall make it; it is pleasant to have needle-work in one's hands while one is listening."

The pinafore was soon cut out from some

pretty white checked muslin which Aunt Pen found for me, and I stitched away very busily while Peep went through his alphabet with so much readiness as to make Aunt Pen say, —

"Come! you know your letters already very well indeed; you'll soon learn to read easily."

Peep looked very much delighted, and he was just beginning to go through the small letters after the capital letters, when we heard the sound of wheels coming along the road and then stop at our garden-gate. We looked out and saw a lady, with a little boy and girl beside her, walking up the path towards the house.

"It's Mabel!" cried Peep.

"It's Jamie!" I said. "It must be their mamma with them."

"Who are they? Who is their mamma?" asked Aunt Pen.

"She's Lady Buckhurst. We know them; we have met them; but we never saw her."

As I spoke, the house-door was opened by Sue, who then opened the parlor-door and showed in the lady and the two children. They both ran straight to us and shook hands with us, while their mamma went up to Aunt Pen and said, —

"I hope, dear Mrs. Bruff, you will forgive the freedom I take in calling upon you so very soon after your coming home; but I felt that I could not let a day pass before I came to thank you for the great help your little people gave mine lately, when, but for their presence of mind, my little Mabel and Jamie might have been drowned."

"Your ladyship is very good, very kind; but I hardly know what you speak of. I rejoice to learn that my little Bab and Peep behaved well; but I have heard nothing of any such accident. The children have had hardly time to tell me yet; I only came home yesterday, and I have but just made their acquaintance, as it were, though they are already dear to me."

"They deserve to be dear to all who know

them; they are good, brave, sensible children, and I am glad to be able to thank them myself. I only waited to do so till I could call upon you and introduce myself properly before I brought my own thanks. Let me do so now. You see the little ones have already made friends together, and understand each other without ceremony. I hope we shall do the same."

"Mamma," said little Jamie, eagerly, "may I take Peep out to see Stubbs and the horses? He says he should like to see them."

His mother nodded and smiled; the two boys ran out to the gate, and Lady Buckhurst went on, —

"I hope we shall become excellent neighbors, Mrs. Bruff. My little people will have charming companions in yours, and they are sadly in want of young company just now, for their elder brother is away at school, and they miss him very much; yet it is not every child that I like mine to be intimate with, as I wish them only to have for young friends

children well brought up in right ideas of
good conduct and honest principles.   I chance
to have heard something of the excellent be-
havior of your young folk in particular cir-
cumstances that I will relate to you some day
or other; and I tell you frankly, they are
just the companions and playfellows I should
like to secure for my Mabel and Jamie.   Shall
it be so?   Will you let them come to Buckhurst Park?"

"I shall be only too glad, and they, I
know, will be delighted to come."

"Then we have only to fix the day, and I
hope you will let it be an early one, and come
and spend the whole day with us.   As the
Park is some distance from here, I hope you
will let me send the carriage for you.   Shall
it be to-morrow, or the day after?"

"You are very good, very thoughtful, Lady
Buckhurst; but — "

"My dear Mrs. Bruff, excuse my interrupting you, but why need there be a 'but'
in this case?"

"Your ladyship has been so obliging as

to speak frankly to me ; will you allow me to speak frankly to you ? "

"Certainly ; I ask nothing better."

" Well, then, I hope you will let me send the children to the park to spend the day, and permit me to stay at home."

" Do you feel not strong yet ? I hear you have been ill and greatly tried. I would not press you to come if you still feel unequal to the exertion. But a drive in the open air, a stroll in the garden, the park, I hope, might even do you good."

" It is not that. I think it would be most pleasant, most healthful ; but — I told you I would speak frankly — you see me the wife of Captain Bruff ; he is of a good family, so even am I ; but perhaps you do not know that I have been a poor needle-woman, working for my daily bread, and I should not like you hereafter to discover this, and perhaps regret — so well am I acquainted with the conventional rules of society — that you had sought the acquaintance of one who has held so low a position in the world."

" My dear Mrs. Bruff, as we *are* frank with each other, you know, I must say you make me smile at your over-delicacy; and yet I admire you the more for it. In a village place like this, we get to know all ' how and about' everybody, and I have long known all ' how and about' the good devoted daughter who earned bread for her dear mother and herself independently and nobly, instead of being a burden upon her richer relations; how she may have been a ' poor needlewoman,' an industrious seamstress, — what you will, — but how she was always the born gentlewoman, the innate gentlewoman, the gentlewoman in heart as well as by birth."

I saw a look of bright joy flash out of Aunt Pen's soft eyes as Lady Buckhurst said this, then shook her warmly by the hand, and ended by kissing her cordially on the cheek.

" My dear Mrs. Bruff, I mean always to be as frank and candid as I am now. It is my nature to speak out openly; I even do so before my children, — not being of opinion, with many people, that there should be re-

serves in their presence, as I think it well
they should early be taught the truth with
respect to worldly rank, position, and real
dignity. I will tell you, at once, that I am
less well-born than yourself. I was a hard-
working governess when Sir James Buckhurst married me, and my relations were
hard-working commercial people, not particularly wealthy. I wish they had been, for a
rich dowry with his wife would have been
useful to my dear Sir James, who, though
descended from one of the oldest families in
the county, had his paternal estate so much
injured by the extravagance of his forefathers
that he has been obliged to practise the strict-
est economy to keep the old place still in his
own possession. Therefore you will find us
with antique furniture, faded carpets and curtains, but with a certain grace and beauty of
bygone mode about it all which I think will
have its charm for you as well as I own it has
for me. Come and judge for yourself as soon
as may be. Let me say the day after to-
morrow, — Saturday; and meantime, pray

forgive me for this unconscionably long first call."

She stepped into her carriage with her frank, winning smile, leaving us all delighted with herself and her visit.

## CHAPTER XV.

WHEN Saturday came, it was as brilliant a morning as could be wished; and though there was a fresh, crisp air, yet the sun shone out, giving warmth and a feeling of actual spring to the still early season. The carriage came in excellent time, as appointed, during the forenoon; so that we children had not much trial of our patience after we were ready dressed a good quarter of an hour before we need have been. Peep asked if he might sit on the coach-box with Stubbs; so that Aunt Pen and I had the inside of the carriage all to ourselves, and we could loll back on the soft-cushioned seats and play at being great ladies to our hearts' content. She humored me in my fancy, and called herself

the Duchess of Airs-and-Graces, while address-
ing me as Marchioness Mincing-Mouth; and
we talked to each other in the most prim,
stiff, ridiculous tone and absurd manner.
Then she broke off, laughing, and said, —

"Ay, it's all very well to do this for fun;
but, really, the best-bred people are, in fact,
generally the most easy and unaffected."

The carriage had passed through the village, and was now in a pretty little country
lane, where the hedges were beginning to be
covered with light green tips and tufts of
scarcely opened leaves; the slender blades
of grass beneath the hedges were of the most
exquisite tint, and suddenly, peering among
them, I called out, —

"Oh, look, look, Aunty! There's a speck
of bluish color; I do believe it's a vio-
let! And, oh, look! There are some primroses. I do wish we were walking instead
of driving! I could gather some to take to
Mabel."

"Ah, Bab, you see even being in a carriage
may have its drawbacks, eh?"

"Yes, Aunty. I wonder whether we might tell Stubbs to stop a moment while I get out and pick a little nosegay of violets and primroses. Do you think I might?"

"Well, my dear, I think it will not be polite to linger on our way, when we are paying our first visit, and gathering wild flowers takes up time in a wonderful way; we go on from one to another, and finding 'just this one more,' and, 'oh, just this other little beauty,' till hours melt before we are aware."

"Oh, yes, I know, exactly; it's quite true; you're right, Aunty."

Just then the carriage turned through some ivy-covered gates in the midst of a moss-grown paling that enclosed the park for some miles round. There was a mellow browny-gray look about this wooden enclosure itself which made its coating of velvety moss and the ferns and docks at its foot form so beautiful an effect that both Aunty and I burst out with, —

"Oh, how very, very lovely!"

"I say, Bab," shouted Peep, "did you ever see such a place? Look up at these grand old trees over our heads!"

We were passing along a noble avenue of elms, and on either side we saw groups of tall oaks, ashes, beeches (for Aunty told me their names), in threes and twos, or more, together; while in the glades between we saw slants of sunshine, and soft shadows and distant peeps of blue hills.

"Oh, Bab!" screamed Peep, "look there! Deer! stags! Oh, look at their branching horns! Look at their light brown sides, some of them spotted underneath with white!"

"Yes; 'antlers,' you know, Peep, and 'dappled coats,' that father used to tell us deer had. Do you remember?"

"Oh, yes; and to think, Bab, that we really see deer ourselves, at last! Oh, look, quick! I see something of bright light blue dart across! A bird! a beautiful bird!"

"A jay, with its jewelled wing," said Aunt Pen.

"Jewelled, Aunty?" I said wonderingly.
"Can birds wear jewels?"

Aunt Pen laughed, and said, —

"Some birds seem made of jewels, — the
jay with its wing like a sapphire; the king-
fisher, the humming-bird, that look as if
rubies and emeralds and amethysts were
clustered together upon their throats and
breasts."

As she spoke, we drove up to the edge of
a broad stone terrace on which the house
stood. There was a fountain at one end of
this terrace and a sun-dial at the other; and
the, stone of the terrace and the fountain
and the antique dial was grass-grown, moss-
grown, and softened by this green coloring.
Before we had got well out of the carriage,
Lady Buckhurst, Mabel, and Jamie came out
upon the terrace to meet us. They welcomed
us in the heartiest way, and led us into a fine
spacious hall that reached from the ground-
floor up to the very top of the house. This
hall was hung round with old armor and
ancient weapons, with stags' antlers, and bows

15

and arrows, and fowling-pieces, and fishing-rods; with tall Indian vases in the corners, from which a delicious smell of lavender and rose-leaves came and filled the air of the hall with a delicate, hoarded-up kind of scent, like old drawers full of lace and muslin that mother used to tell me about; and high up, round the hall, there was a railed-in gallery, in one recess of which there was an organ, with its rows of metal pipes and its rich, dark front of wood. Some of these things I noticed at once; others I remembered afterwards, when Aunty talked them over with me after our first visit. From the hall we turned into a small room which Lady Buckhurst told us was where Sir James saw his tenants and farm-people, and which adjoined his own study. On entering the small room, we saw a young girl standing waiting, who dropped a courtesy when we came in. Lady Buckhurst asked her who she was, and the girl answered :

" If you please, my lady, I 'm Jenny Sparks; father sent me to Sir James to tell him — to ask him — "

"Sir James is gone out riding this morning, my girl, but he will be home soon after one, and he will see you then, and hear what you have to say to him from your father."

"Yes, mylady; the footman told me so, and bade me wait here till Sir James returns."

We went on into the delightful little study, which was fitted up with shelves full, full of books, — a lowish range of shelves, over which were busts and statuettes on oaken brackets, and engravings hung round in simple oak frames.

"Sir James amuses himself with making his brackets and frames with his own hands, from the trees in the park," said Lady Buckhurst. "It saves cost, and it gives pleasant occupation, — a double good."

She showed us through many charming rooms, — one long drawing-room, where there were some fine old family portraits and good paintings, and where we lingered some time enjoying the pictures — until we came into a nice shady homey-looking room, where needle-work, and embroidery frames, and workbaskets, and books that looked as if they were lying there to be read between whiles were in just that pleasant confusion which does n't look untidy, but only looks like comfortable ease. Here Lady Buckhurst made us sit down and rest till lunch-time; there being endless sofas and arm-chairs and low cushioned seats, covered with a pretty flowered chintz.

" Very old-fashioned, you see, as I told you; but very cosey and enjoyable, I think. I should be sorry to see anything modernized in this dear old place, this old-world, go-to-sleep, behind-the-age nook of ours."

" Nothing could be in worse taste than to alter a single long-established decoration here," said Aunt Pen, " where all is in harmony of antiquated grace and beauty."

" Mabel, my darling, go and tell Mrs. Quince that I wish her not to wait till papa comes home, but to send in lunch at once, as I think our friends will be hungry after their drive through the open air. And, Mabel, you can take your little friend with you, as she may like to see the housekeeper's room, and the store-cupboards, and the glass-closets, and all Mrs. Quince's orderly ways, as well as Mrs. Quince herself, who is quite a character, and looks like an old picture stepped from its canvas."

Lady Buckhurst said this last to Aunty, while Mabel and I ran off to the old house-keeper, whom we found looking the very pink of neatness, in a close mob-cap, which had a quilling of net that went round her face and under her chin, and with a snowy muslin kerchief folded across her bosom, and a large white muslin apron over her dark stuff gown. When Mabel had delivered her mother's message, she said, —

"Mrs. Quince, you dear old duck, I want to coax you to let me put together a plate of cakes and fruit and sweeties for Bab and me to take to papa's morning-room, where there is a young girl waiting to speak to him, who looked pale and thin and tired with her long walk and her long waiting; and I should so like to take her something that would help to pass the time till papa comes home."

"Ah, Miss Mabel, Miss Mabel, you know well enough I can never help letting you have your own way, or anything you want. There are the cakes, my dear, here are the sweets and goodies, and here's the fruit on this shelf."

She opened her stores and displayed them with evident pride in their orderly arrangement. Mabel took two plates, and arranged a pile of dainties on each, giving me one to carry and carrying the other herself.

"Now give me a sheet of nice, stout, white paper, Quincey dear, and then I shall have all I want, and we'll be off out of your way."

"Out of *my* way when you've had *yours*, eh, Miss Mabel? Ah, just like all you children. Well, it's natural, it's natural, and I've nothing to say against it; for what's natural's natural, of course, and I'm not one to go against nature, so there's an end of the matter."

We carried our platesful very carefully, and succeeded in conveying them without toppling off anything, straight along the passage

from the housekeeper's room, across the large
hall and into the small morning-room. As
Mabel set down her plate to open the door,
and I was balancing mine between both my
hands, I heard a rustle and quick rush across
the room we were entering; but when Mabel
took up her plate again and she and I went
in, side by side together, we found the young
girl standing just where we had found her
when we first saw her. I noticed that her
face, which had been very white then, looked
very red now. However, she dropped her
courtesy as before, and seemed struck dumb
with surprise when Mabel and I put the
plates before her, Mabel saying, —

"I thought you looked tired, and would be
still more tired waiting so long; therefore
we've brought you some nice things to pass
the time, and I thought you'd perhaps like to
have this sheet of paper and make a parcel of
what you didn't care to eat here, and take it
home with you to give to your little brothers
and sisters, if you have any. Have you?"

"Six," was the short answer.

Then the girl seemed to think it too short, and she flurriedly said, —

"Six, miss."

She looked staringly and rather bewilderedly at Mabel; then she dropped another courtesy, and said, —

"Thank you! Oh, thank you, Miss! How good of you — how good of you to think of bringing these!"

"Good-by; I hope you'll enjoy them. Come, Bab, we must fly back to mamma. Lunch will be ready."

## CHAPTER XVI.

E had such a pretty lunch! Almost as many wild flowers on the table as dishes of cream-cheese and fruit and cakes and preserves. There were violets, primroses, daffodils, daisies, mosses, and delicate grasses, placed in very simple but very beautifully shaped vases and glasses, which my Aunt admired extremely.

"Sir James and I always agree that what we have in daily use need not be costly to be elegant; and often the most really pretty things are the least expensive. I remember once seeing an exquisite little green basket-dish of the very commonest earthenware which my lady friend, who brought it from a village in Italy, on the Adriatic, told me cost but a few pence; and yet it was perfectly fashioned, and looked like a firm open plait of

green rushes rounded into a receptacle for
fruit, which she used constantly among her
dessert service. By the way, you see I give
you nothing more than bread and cheese and
fruit for lunch, as I want you to eat a good
dinner, which I have ordered rather early, so
that you may drive home before dark, and
not let Captain Bruff be left too long without you all."

She chatted on gayly and brightly during
and after lunch, so that time passed almost
unperceived, until at length she said, —

"It is rather strange Sir James is not yet
returned; it must be long past the hour he
said he would be back."

"And that poor girl, Jenny Sparks, must
be still waiting, waiting, mamma," said Mabel. "I'm so glad Bab and I thought of
taking her something to help her pass away
the time. It must have seemed very long,
even then, when I first saw her and noticed
how pale and tired she looked."

"But she did n't look pale when we took
her the plates of nice things. She looked

very red, and she looked very odd, — somehow very startled and disturbed."

"Perhaps she had fallen asleep, tired of waiting," said Mabel.

"No, I don't think she had been sleeping," I said. "I thought I heard something stir when you opened the door; something like a hurrying across the room, — a hasty step."

"Your little Bab is a very noticing little person, strangely observant for one so young," said Lady Buckhurst, smiling at Aunt Pen. "But if you are quite rested we will go back to the hall, and I can let you hear the fine tone of our organ; and we will take a peep at the poor, patient, long-waiting girl at the same time, and see whether she is asleep or awake now."

We all went, as she proposed; and before going up into the organ-gallery, Lady Buckhurst softly opened the door of the small morning-room and looked in. The girl had flung herself down upon one of the chairs, her hands clasped over her face; but she started up with a slight scream as she heard us approach. She burst into a passion of sobs, and looked violently agitated as she said, —

"Oh, mylady, forgive me, forgive me! Though I can't forgive myself hardly; but I 'll tell you the whole truth, indeed, indeed I will!"

"If you tell me the whole truth, I certainly shall forgive you; if you tell me the exact truth, — the exact truth, mind, — I promise to be not even very angry with you."

"Oh, mylady, I did n't mean to do wrong! I did n't think of it, it did n't come into my mind to do it, till, after waiting a good hour for Sir James, I grew tired of staying in this one room and I just gave a peep into the next. I found it full, oh, so full of books; I 'd never seen so many together before in my life; I did n't think there 'd been so many books in all the world, mylady; and then I began to take one of them down from the shelf, to see if there were any pictures in it; but there were n't, and as I put it back in its place my eye caught a queer little figure on the table, — a figure of a boy with wings on his shoulders and his finger to his lips; and it was bright and shining, like silver, and I thought it *was* silver, and I saw it was perched on the top of the lid to a thing made to hold ink, and I found the lid came off quite easily when I touched it, — for I did touch it, mylady, oh, I did touch it! And then the thought came into my head what a pretty thing it was, and how I should like to show it to brothers and sisters at home. Before I hardly knew what I did, mylady, I put it in my pocket; but indeed I did n't take it because it was silver. Indeed, indeed, I did n't *steal* it! I did n't take it for its value, mylady; do believe that!"

"It is not silver; it is not of value excepting for its prettiness. So, you see, if you had taken it to sell, you would not have sold it for much; and you would not have been able to sell it without being at once found out, it is so peculiar. But go on."

"I had just put it in my pocket, mylady, when I heard the door open and somebody outside who seemed to be coming in; but before they did, I had time to run back to the place where I had been standing in this room. I had no sooner done so than I saw these two little ladies, each carrying a plate piled up with good things which they had brought for me, — for me, mylady, for *me!* I, who had just been behaving like a thief, and had thought of robbing them, or at least taking away something that belonged to their house. I felt as I'd never felt before, and as I hope I never shall feel again in my life, if I live to be a hundred years old. I was ashamed — ashamed of *myself;* ready to hide under the earth if I could, and stamp it down upon my head. This was after the two little angels — for they looked like angels to me, — had gone away; and then it suddenly darted into my head that I could put back the queer figure with the wings into its place, and nobody would know how wicked I had been. It seemed to burn my pocket, and I felt better when I put it back again; but I could n't feel easy, even though I thought nobody need know anything of it. And now I'm glad you've made me tell you the whole truth, mylady."

"So am I, Jenny; and not only do I forgive you, as I promised I would, but I trust you and believe you. Nay, I even believe that this one severe lesson, and the pain you have gone through, will prevent you from having the least wish to take anything that is not yours as long as you live."

"She hasn't touched one of the nice things, mamma," said Mabel, looking at the two plates. "May I make them up into a parcel for her to take home to her six little brothers and sisters?"

"Yes, my dear. And, Jenny, it is no use waiting any longer to-day for Sir James's return; something has detained him, I dare say. Therefore I will tell them to give you something more substantial to eat than cakes before you go, as you must be nearly famished, I should think, waiting all this time. Goodday, Jenny, and don't forget the lesson you have had."

"No, mylady, never, never! And never

can I forget how good your ladyship's been to me!"

She dropped her courtesy, and her heart seemed too full to say more. Lady Buckhurst rang the bell and gave her orders to the footman, who was followed by Jenny Sparks with a grateful look at us all round as she left the room.

We all went up into the gallery that ran round the hall, and listened to some delightful organ-playing till Sir James came home, and then we all sat down to dinner, — a bright, cheery, gay meal, where Sir James chatted as easily and pleasantly with us as his frank-natured, smiling wife did; so that when the carriage came round to the terrace-steps, our party were all sorry to break up, and the kind, friendly father and mother, with their young children, came out to see us off, saying over and over how glad they were to see us, and how they hoped it would not be long before they saw us again. On arriving at home we found Uncle at the garden-gate looking out for us.

"Well, my Penn'orth, how are you? Not overtired, I hope. Glad to see you here again, I can tell you. They say 'you're come back to me like a bad penny;' but I say 'you're come back to me like a good penny,' — the best I ever had, my lucky penny, my fortunate penny, my own, own Penn'orth, that I can't afford to lose, or scarcely to let out of my sight."

He seemed in high spirits, as if on purpose not to make us fancy he had been feeling lonely or left-at-home while we had been enjoying such a happy holiday; and he asked us everything we had seen, heard, and done, with the liveliest interest, and we repeated it all with such exact telling, that he said he felt as if he had been there and enjoyed it with us.

It struck me often that Uncle was quite a changed man in some things since his marriage; he was so cheery and merry, and seemed so happy in his home now, with Aunt Pen and Peep and me. She made us all feel so much more close to each other and fond of each other, and interested in what the

16

whole family party thought and did. A delightful feeling of being together, and being
glad to be together, seemed to have grown
up in the house since she had become its
second head; and we enjoyed the improve-
ment immensely, though without saying much
about it in words. I sometimes thought how
astonished and pleased Tom would have felt
could he have been at home to see how very
different a step-mother really might be from
what he had made sure she would be. But
Tom was still away at school, and we only
very rarely had letters from him, which
merely said he was well and hoped we were
the same.

One of these letters came from him just
before we were expecting him home for the
Easter holidays; but instead of its telling us
the day he was coming, it told us he was not
thinking of doing so at all. Uncle read out
the letter to us at breakfast, after he had
first read it to himself. The post generally
came in while we were at breakfast, so that
we often had letters read out to us all, now;

though before we had Aunt Pen with us, Uncle used to read his letters only to himself, and then sit looking into the fire without speaking. This was Tom's letter : —

DEAR FATHER, — Dick Wentworth has asked me to spend the Easter holidays at his father's place near here. It's a fine place, he says, and there 'll be lots of fishing and shooting and boating and games, and it 'll be great fun. So I hope you 'll let me go instead of coming home this half, as Dick's father is quite one of the county swells, and he expects a great many London swells at Easter on a visit. I shall want a dress-suit of clothes for evenings and dinner-parties, besides plenty of other things that take cash, and my pocket-money 's running short ; therefore I shall be glad if you 'll be the generous governor I 've always found you, and send a supply to

Your dutiful son,

THOMAS BRUFF.

"Very 'dutiful,' truly!" said Uncle. "'Governor'! 'swells'! How I hate slang! And how the young people use it now-a-days! How hard it sounds, and how hard it makes them! It seems to help them to fling off all feeling,—even the little they might have left; for there's the very smallest quantity remaining, I think, now-a-days."

" Don't say so; there's plenty left in the world," said Aunt Pen, earnestly, " only it's voted old-fashioned to *show* feeling."

" More's the pity, Penn'orth ! I think just a little might have been shown in this very letter, if only for decent civility's sake. Not one word of remembrance to any of us here; not a syllable to show that though he's eager to go and spend his holidays with his school-fellow, he's sorry to have to give up coming to see his old home and all of us here. I could n't have believed Tom was so hard and unfeeling."

" Boys are apt to be thoughtless about sending messages home; and they often seem harder than they really are. They frequently feel a good deal, but think it manly to hide their feelings."

" The most manly men are the most tender-hearted. Look at what Nelson was! No; Tom's only thinking of Dick's father's ' fine place,' the 'lots of fun' he 'll have there, and the extra pocket-money he wants me to send him."

" That his head should be full of the gay holiday he hopes to have, is rather natural, don't you think?   And that he should wish to be provided with enough money to be able to enjoy it properly, is also really very natural, I think; and I 'm sure you 'll think so too, Uncle, when you come to think it over quietly."

Aunt Pen often called him " Uncle," hearing us always call him so; and it came to be her settled name for him.

" Well, well!   I *will* think it over, my Penn'orth, and I dare say I shall end by thinking as you do; for I generally come round to your opinion, finding yours the most sensible and certainly the most kind."

And thus, I afterwards heard, was the case. Uncle sent Tom a handsome extra allowance, wishing him a pleasant holiday this Easter at Wentworth Hall, where he had his full consent to go.

# CHAPTER XVII.

ONE of the many pleasant things that Aunt Pen did for me was to let me feel that I could be useful to her. After breakfast and lessons were over she always let me go with her into the kitchen to give Sue her orders for the day, and then to the store-cupboard to look out stores, and then to the pantry, the linen-cupboard, and the china-cupboard, contriving constantly to find out some little job for me to do to help her. She even sometimes let me do a little shopping for her, when she found that I was proud of being allowed to go out by myself and fetch the things she wanted, and that I quite well knew my way to the shops, and could choose and pay for what I bought without any grown-up person

to help me. One day she happened to want
some darning-cotton and some reels of sewing-
cotton of different fineness and coarseness,
and as she had a batch of apple-jam to make,
she allowed me to go and buy the cottons;
saying she would trust me, with my sharp
eyes, and my knowledge of the qualities she
wanted, to pick them out for her. I went
to the shop where the good-natured young
woman once gave me the pretty scraps I
mentioned, and I always asked her to serve
me when I went there, as she smiled at me
and seemed glad to help me in my purchases.
On this day I was glad to find her disengaged
and able to attend to me, and she was patiently helping me to choose out the fine and
the coarse skeins and reels for Aunt, when a
carriage stopped at the shop-door and a very
smartly dressed lady came in with rather an
important manner and an ordering voice,
though it was a drawling voice too. I knew
it at once, and I knew her; but she did not
notice me, and I think did not even see who
I was, for I stood close to the counter, look-

ing carefully into the two box-drawers placed before me to choose from.

" Is Mrs. Pinkins in the way ?   Tell her to come and wait upon me; I like the shop-mistress herself to serve me.   Let her know Mrs. Botterby is here."

" Yes, ma'am, immegiate ; certainly, ma'am."

One of the young shopwomen hurried away and soon returned with Mrs. Pinkins, who came bustling and smirking and cour-tesying, to show Mrs. Botterby some silks and ribbons that she asked for.

While she was pulling over and having shown to her roll after roll of ribbon, and looking at length after length of various col-ored silks, I went on with my picking out cottons, both of which took some time; but still she did n't turn her eyes towards me. She sat on one of the high shop-chairs with her back a little turned from where I stood close beside her, now and then drawing a ribbon through her fingers, or trying the thickness of one of the showy silks that lay at last in a heap before her.

" What did you say was the price of this checked pink-and-brown ? "

" Eight and sixpence a yard, ma'am."

" And this red and olive ? "

" Same price, ma'am. They 're the last thing out in checked silks, and not dear, I think you 'll say, ma'am, if you consider their quality, and that they 're quite the last fashion."

" Oh, price is not an object with me, Mrs. Pinkins. I was only thinking which was most becoming when made up, — the dark or the light check. Price, you know, is the last thing that weighs with me."

" Of course, ma'am. We all know that the lady of the rich Mr. Botterby — you 'll excuse me, ma'am, but that 's the name you go by hereabouts — need n't look to price in an article she takes a liking to. Here 's this gray satinet, it 's nine-and-six a yard; and though it 's so delicate in color, it 'll wear well, it 's so good in quality."

" Oh, as to wearing well, that 's little consequence with me, you know."

"To be sure, ma'am, of course; but what I mean is, it's a lady-like, elegant silk. Captain Bruff lately bought a length for his bride."

"Oh, by the bye, Mrs. Pinkins, I hear you've a new neighbor settled here. What sort of a person is she? Somewhere I heard that she was a mere nobody, — a seamstress, a girl who took in plain needle-work for her living. What in the name of wonder made the man marry her? What luck those creatures have, have n't they?"

Mrs. Pinkins did n't seem to notice me any more than Mrs. Botterby did; but I saw the young woman who was serving me get rather red and cast a glance at my face. I suppose she thought I did n't hear what was going on, for I kept on steadily looking at the cottons.

"It was a good catch for her, to be sure, ma'am," was Mrs. Pinkins's answer; "and to think of the captain's buying that lady-like rich silk for a dress for her! It's a beauty, is n't it, ma'am?"

"Well, Mrs. Pinkins, it's rather too quiet

and dowdy to suit my taste. I like something more handsome-looking. What have you in brocades?"

"Here are some just out, ma'am; here 's one — but it 's eleven-and-six the yard — quite in your way, ma'am. It 'd make a very stylish dinner-dress, — yellow, spotted with dead-leaf colored sprigs."

"Yes, very pretty; 1 think I 'll decide for a length of that one. But what sort of a *looking* person is this new Mrs. Bruff? Is she pretty? 1 suppose so, or he would n't have thought of her for a wife, of course. Is she anything in manners? Does she know how to behave? Is she fit to mix in society? Because, you must know, Mrs. Pinkins, my daughter Almeria — Miss Botterby, you know — happened to meet the children — the niece and nephew, I believe they are — of this Captain Bruff; and before I let her follow up the acquaintance, — for she took rather a fancy to them, — I should like to know whether his wife 's the sort of person one would care to invite or to call upon."

"Oh, ma'am, I've always heard she's quite respectable; not a word against her, though it's quite true she took in needle-work and earned her own livelihood."

"Oh, yes, respectable, I dare say; worthy, and all that. But what I mean is, are her manners good? Does she seem fit for her new position?"

"Well, ma'am, to tell you the truth, I've never seen her yet. Whenever she's come to the shop, it so chanced that I was not in the way. For I mostly don't serve myself; I leave it to the young women; and Mr. Pinkins don't care for me to attend much to the business except when pa'tic'lar kind of ladies — like you, Mrs. Botterby, who are one of our very best customers — come into the place. How many yards shall I say, ma'am?"

"Twenty yards; stay, perhaps you'd better cut twenty-two; dresses take so much stuff now-a-days, and I like my trains *very* long. But as to this Mrs. Bruff, I really want to know something about her that I can rely upon. Do you know any one near here who *can* tell me what she is?"

"I can!" I said, in a quiet but distinct tone. Mrs. Botterby looked sharply round.

"And who may you be, child? Oh, I see, Captain Bruff's little girl."

"His niece," I said.

"And you heard all I have been saying to Mrs. Pinkins, I suppose?"

"I was so close to you, I could not help hearing."

"Well, no great harm. I said nothing that I care about being overheard."

"You said she was a mere nobody, a seamstress, a girl who took in plain needle-work for her living."

"Well, I did say so; and so she did, did n't she?"

"Yes, and she told Lady Buckhurst she did; and then Lady Buckhurst said she might have been a poor needle-woman, but she was a born gentlewoman, — a gentlewoman in heart and mind."

"Lady Buckhurst said so? When?"

" When she called to see us, and asked us to go and see her at Buckhurst Park."

" Called ?   Did Lady Buckhurst call upon Mrs. Bruff ?   Did she ask her to go and see her at Buckhurst Park ? "

" Yes; she invited us all to go and see her there, and we spent — oh, such a pleasant day ! "

" Dear me !   Lady Buckhurst calling, Lady Buckhurst inviting her up to the Park, — that makes an immense difference."

Mrs. Botterby stopped short in her speech and seemed to be thinking.   Then she suddenly said, —

" After all, one has a right to be very particular as to who's who, you know, Mrs. Pinkins, when one's children's visitors or one's own visitors are the question.   One likes to know who one makes acquaintance with in a country neighborhood; one can't be too careful."

" Quite so, ma'am; and since Lady Buckhurst sets the example, why — "

" Oh, as to Lady Buckhurst, — well, she has

married into one of the oldest county families; so of course she's received and thought
a great deal of. But even her ladyship, —
between you and me, Mrs. Pinkins, I *have*
heard that she herself, before her marriage,
was only a governess, — a governess; actually
nothing more than a governess!"

Mrs. Botterby had dropped her voice to a
whisper as she said this, leaning over the
counter and saying it quite low to Mrs. Pinkins; but I distinctly heard her words, and I
saw Mrs. Pinkins glance towards me and
whisper, in return, something about " Little
pitchers have long ears, you know, ma'am;"
and then Mrs. Botterby nodded, saying, —

" Yes, indeed ; I never saw such a child for
noticing and hearing everything; really, I
never did."

Then she turned round to me and said, —

" My daughter Almeria often talks of you
and your little brother, and wishes you'd
come and see her again. Will you?"

" I will ask Aunt Pen if she will let me
come," I answered.

" Let you come, child ? Why, of course she will. She 'll be only too glad you should visit at Botterby House."

" I 'll ask her. Good morning," I said.

Then, having chosen all the darning and sewing cottons Aunty wanted, I went out of the shop.

On reaching home, and having given her the cottons and hearing her say I had done my commission like a nice little clever woman who knew how to do shopping as if she were grown up, I told Aunt Pen all I had seen and heard at Mrs. Pinkins's.

She listened quietly to all I had to tell her, and seemed much amused as I went on. But when I came to Mrs. Botterby's invitation, she asked me what I felt about it, and whether I wished to accept.

" I don't think I should care to go to Botterby House again, Aunty ; Miss Botterby is a very good-natured girl, and I should n't like to be ungrateful to her for her kindness, for she *meant* to be kind and generous when she had that beautiful doll's hood and cloak made for me; but some things make me not like her or her mamma. I don't like Mrs. Botterby's saying what she did of you, or her *manner* of saying it, in the first place; and in the second place — "

" As far as what she said of me, Bab, it's of no consequence; it's true, you know: I *was* a needle-woman; and she has a right to decide whether she'll call upon me and ask me to visit her, or not, just as she pleases. What I should like to find out is, whether *you* wish to visit there."

" Well, Aunty, I'll try and explain all I feel about this. I must begin by telling you the whole story of Peep's and my meeting Miss Botterby, and then our going to see her."

" You went to see her? You've been to Botterby House already? But tell me the whole story, — tell it me all through."

I did so; and then I said, —

" You see, Aunty, though Miss Botterby meant kindly, she behaved slyly and disagreeably; and though her mamma is civil to me,

17

she seems to me to be, for all her fine house
and her fine gardens and hot-houses, and her
fine clothes, and her great riches, to be a very
— a very — I don't know exactly how to say
it, but I know what I mean.   Of course, she
is n't common and vulgar in the way that
people in the streets, or in the poor cottages,
are common and vulgar; but somehow Mrs.
Botterby seems to be a very vulgar woman.
Do you understand me, Aunt Pen?"

"Yes, my dear, quite.   You find her vulgar-
minded, and she is so; and certainly her
daughter, though kind-hearted perhaps, is
full of sly, unworthy ways.   I don't think
visiting at Botterby House will either be very
pleasant to you or very good for you.   Still,
we must n't be churlish to our neighbors when
they want to be polite to us; and if Mrs. Botterby calls here, we will be as civil as we can
to her while she pays her visit; and if we
meet her anywhere else, we can also be civil
for our own sakes as ladies.   But we can
avoid regular visits to Botterby House."

# CHAPTER XVIII.

 DAY was fixed for our going again to Buckhurst Park, when we were to walk instead of drive, in order that we might more thoroughly enjoy the beauties of the trees and glades; but it vexatiously happened that poor Aunty had one of her bad headaches that morning, and she felt unequal to go. Uncle, before he went away to town, made her promise that she would not attempt it, and she readily promised, saying that she would lie down quietly as soon as he was gone; hoping that silence and darkness would cure her by the time he came back in the evening.

"And as I shall be glad not to have to talk or give lessons to-day, I think the chicks may be allowed to go to Buckhurst Park by themselves, and not be disappointed of their day there, after all."

" A very good thought, my Penn'orth! Just like one of yours! Off with you, Bab and Peep; and mind you don't get into any scrapes by the way!"

Though we were sorry not to have Aunt Pen with us, Peep and I enjoyed our walk immensely. First, it was a delicious spring day, mild and sunny; then our road lay through such lovely scenery that at every step there was something to admire. On entering the ivy-covered Park gates and finding ourselves in the noble avenue, we felt almost as if we were going into a large, long church, with rows of tall columns, and a soft green light up among its arches and high roof; and we walked on for a little while without saying a word. Suddenly Peep called out, —

"Bab, Bab, see there! What's that little, bright, brown creature scampering across the grass? See, it's making for those four big trees over there!"

" Oh, it's a squirrel! Look at its bushy

tail, and its smooth up-and-down body as it runs! Oh, it has reached the trees and is climbing up one of them, oh, so quickly, darting from branch to branch! And now it's up at the top; see how it peeps down at us as if laughing at our not being able to follow it up there!"

We both ran towards the tree to see if we could still watch the squirrel, who had popped his head behind one of the top branches, after peeping at us from it; and while we were walking round and round the tree, peering up, Peep had not noticed a tall stag that came slowly up one of the green glades and then stood stock-still, gazing at us.

"Peep," I whispered, "look at that deer! What huge branching horns he has! How he stares at us! Perhaps he's angry at our coming so near his trees; do you think he is?"

"No, Bab, of course not; he's only looking at us, as we're looking at him. You're trembling; are you afraid?"

"Yes; he looks so grave, and stares at us so steadily."

"Well, stand still, don't attempt to run. Keep your eyes fixed on him. I recollect father said that if you tried to run from an animal, they were sure to run after you and attack you; but that if you looked them full in the face, and kept your eyes fixed upon theirs, they could n't stand it, and would very likely turn and run away."

"But he don't look as if he meant to run away; he never stirs."

"Keep up your courage, and keep looking at him, and don't move!"

"My knees are shaking so, I can hardly stand up."

"Try, try, Bab! Hold still as long as ever you can. Don't fall if you can possibly help it. Bulls sometimes trample you to death, if they see you drop on the ground. Be courageous, Bab; you generally are, you know. Remember how you were praised for presence of mind and courage when we helped the children out of the pond. I can't bear to feel you tremble. Don't give way!"

Even in that moment, when I was so ter-

ribly afraid, I felt proud of Peep's boldness,
and was glad to have him beside me, little
fellow as he was. All of a sudden he snatched
off his cap and threw it smack in the tall
stag's face, who gave a start backwards, turned
round, and lightly bounded away to join the
herd of deer that were at a little distance. I
could n't help bursting into a ridiculous gig-
gle of laughter, though tears were pouring
down my cheeks at the same time, as I sank
down on the grass and shivered all over.

"Nonsense, Bab, don't do that! You
frighten *me*, now, crying and laughing at
once. Don't, don't!"

But I could n't stop myself, and poor Peep
looked at me in helpless bewilderment. Just
then there came in sight three figures, who,
immediately they saw us, ran eagerly towards
the spot where we were. It proved to be
Mabel and Jamie, with another boy, older than
they.

"Why, what's the matter, Bab and Peep?
You're looking as scared as if you'd seen a
wild beast, — a lion or a tiger."

"We've seen nearly as bad," said Peep; "we've met a large stag who looked as if he were going to drive his antlers into us for daring to come too near him; and Bab got timid, and I got frightened seeing her shiver and laugh and cry in this strange way. Look, she can hardly keep from it now!"

"Stay, give me your hand; I'll help you up from the grass, and then lean upon my arm while I take you a few steps from here, where there's a little mossy fountain with a fresh clear spring of water, and some of that will soon set you to rights. Come!"

The boy — who spoke with a bright, cheery tone, and whose face was the most pleasant and beaming I had ever seen — I guessed directly must be Mabel's and Jamie's elder brother William, now come home from school for the Easter holidays.

"I seem to know you both quite well already, Bab and Peep," he said; "I've heard so much about you from them all at home in their letters to me. By the bye, what an odd name you have, Peep! I suppose you weren't

christened so; what's your real name? Not
but what I like your name of Peep, it's so
quaint and queer and pleasant."

"My real name's Peter; but I've always
been called Peep. What's yours? Oh, yes,
I've heard them speak of you by it; it's
William, isn't it?"

"Yes; but here's the fountain; just hold
your hand in a hollow, cup-like shape, dip it
down into the water, and sip it gently."

I did so, and soon was quite better, and
able to chat with the rest, feeling grateful to
William for his nice thoughtful way of not
noticing me too much, but talking on cheerily
to draw off attention from me while I
couldn't keep from that absurd laughing and
crying together. He had a delightful manner with him, — manly, yet not seeming as if
he fancied himself older or more clever than
we younger ones, and I took a great liking
to him at once. So did Peep, who talked as
freely and easily to William as if he'd been
just the same age as himself. Leading us
to a tempting-looking mossy seat beside the

fountain, William answered many questions
that Peep asked him about the different trees
that stood near the spot, telling him their
names, and what the wood of each was generally used for. At last Peep, pointing to a
grand old oak that had beautiful wide-spread-
ing boughs and a huge rugged trunk, with
wooden steps sticking out from its sides, asked
William what they were for.

" They are for the gamekeepers and wood-
men to climb up easily into the tree when
they want to be hidden among the boughs to
watch the deer at particular seasons of the
year. It is called a Forester's tree, and there
are several of them about the Park. Look,
how easy and convenient they are."

And William jumped up from his seat, ran
to the tree, set his foot on the lowest step,
and had soon mounted them all, till he seated
himself astride one of the topmost branches
and looked down at us, his bright eyes and
his curly brown hair making me think of the
squirrel we had lately seen in just such a position. When he came down he made us tell

him all about the meeting with the stag; and
when I had finished, he said, —

"Well done, Peep! You're a brave boy!
You've plenty of pluck, as the fellows say at
our school; and you'll be a credit to everybody that knows you, when you're a man."

"That he will!" said Mabel. "I do love
bravery in a boy. Jamie often makes me feel
proud of him, he's so courageous; and Bab
feels the same of you, Peep, I know she does."

"Yes. When Peep held my hand so tight
and told me to keep up, and then flung his
cap right at the stag's eyes, I was almost glad
in the very midst of my fright."

"Peep's a hero!" said William, heartily;
"and we'll toast him after dinner, that we
will!"

"Toast me? Roast me?" asked Peep,
with such a puzzled look that we all burst out
laughing.

"No, neither roast you nor baste you;
neither make fun of you nor give you a beating. We'll only drink your health with all
the honors. Hip, hip, hurrah! Here's Peep

the brave, Peep the hero! And the ladies —
my mother and our sisters — shall pledge us
with ringing cheers."

By this time we had left the mossy seat
and were walking on towards the house, — the
three boys a little in advance, rather more
quickly, and looking at a dozen things that
caught their attention and had to be noticed
along the avenue path, while Mabel and I
followed quietly, chatting together.

"I am always so glad when William's at
home," she said. "He's such a capital brisk
fellow, and such a capital companion; he tells
us about his school and his schoolfellows, but
he does n't seem so wrapped up in them that
he can talk of nothing else, as some boys do;
he lets us see that though he enjoys the fun
and frolic and bustle of school, yet that he
likes his dear old home and all of us still better, and does n't think himself above playing
with Jamie and me, for all we're so much
younger than he is."

"How old is he? How much younger are
you two?"

" Oh, he 's past twelve, and we 're only six and eight. One of the things that makes us so glad when William 's at home is, we can have rounds together."

" Rounds ? "

" Yes, rounds; don't you know what rounds are ? "

" Well, I suppose they 're not squares, at least."

Mabel laughed her merry little sweet-toned laugh, and then said, —

" Rounds are musical pieces for three or more voices; and my mother teaches them to William and Jamie and me to sing together when he 's at home. While he 's away she practises them with us two younger ones ready for William's return in the holidays."

" I wish I could hear you sing them."

" You shall, if you like ; we generally sing some for my father after lunch, and my mother beats time."

" What 's that ? What does ' beating time ' mean ? "

" Oh, you 'll see when we sing our rounds.

She moves her hand,—just putting it down lightly at the first of the bar, and waving it to the right and then to the left for the other beats of the bar."

I looked at Mabel, I suppose, with such a droll look of not understanding, that she again gave her pretty little laugh; till the boys turned round and asked us what made us girls so merry. We told them, and we all five went laughing on together till we reached the terrace. Here we lingered a few minutes more to look at the sun-dial, while William explained the figures and lines upon it, and showed us how it let people know exactly the time of day so long as the sun was shining; and then he pointed out the pretty motto carved round the dial,—" I note only the bright hours."

Sir James and Lady Buckhurst made us very welcome; and after lunch we had the promised rounds, — the three children singing several, among which I thought, " When the rosy morn appearing," " Wind, gentle evergreen," " How great is the pleasure," and

" Hark, the merry Christ Church bells," were the prettiest. Lady Buckhurst kindly told us that singing rounds was not very difficult; and asking if Peep and I had any voice, said she would show us how to take part in them. We said we had a little, and could sing one or two little tunes and songs.

" Well, songs are very pretty, and I hope you'll sing us yours, we shall like to hear them; but rounds are still more amusing when three or four singers are in company."

She then showed us how rounds are sung, and taught Peep and me, at once, two very easy rounds, " White sand and gray sand " and " Turn again, Whittington," which we both much enjoyed singing with William, Mabel, and Jamie, — I joining Mabel and Peep joining Jamie, while William's stronger voice did very well alone in his part.

## CHAPTER XIX.

HEN the rounds were finished, we children all went out into the garden, where there was a swing between two tall trees.

"William carpentered it all himself, and put it up, with the help of the gardener," said Mabel. "My father has given William one of the outhouses as his workshop, and he carpenters there many a useful and pretty thing for us all. He made my mother a work-table, and my father a set of library shelves, and Jamie a wheelbarrow, and me a doll's bedstead."

"Oh, have you got a wheelbarrow?" said Peep. "Uncle gave me one,—one that I believe was first made for you, Jamie; but the man said you'd changed your mind for a four-wheeled cart; which was very comfort-

able for me, as I wanted a wheelbarrow beyond everything, and immediately."

"Yes, and very comfortable for me; for
William said he thought he could manage to
make me the wheelbarrow, and so I got both."

We were very happy laughing and talking,
while William swung us high, high, high.
At first I was a little bit afraid to find myself
flying up among the tree-tops; but when I
saw how unfrightened Peep and Jamie and
even Mabel were, I got to like it excessively.
They two only swung a little, letting Peep
and me have the most of the swinging, as it
was quite new to us; and as for William, he
never got into the swing at all himself, but
only swung us. Such an unselfish boy we
found him from the first; and so polite and
kind to their visitors they all were!

After we had had as much swinging as we
liked, they took us to a part of the grounds
where there was a target set up. William
fetched bows and arrows, and we had a try
to shoot at the mark. Jamie was a capital
aimer, and hit the target right in the midst

18

several times; so did Mabel, for they both
said they had been practising hard every day
lately, to be able to surprise William when he
came home from school. Peep succeeded so
well in one or two aims he took, that William
shouted out, "Bravo! bravo! Peep the
hero!"

At dinner Peep's health was drunk, as William had said it should be; and both Sir James
and Lady Buckhurst were interested with the
story of our meeting the stag, which William
made me repeat to them.

We took dessert in the drawing-room, where
the groups of fruit looked like paintings,
spread on a table underneath those fine old
pictures, and where the windows looked out
upon the green lawns and noble trees of the
Park. While we ate some delicious red-
cheeked apples and bronzy-colored pears,
and cracked some filberts, her mother told
Mabel to let us hear a Gay's Fable or two;
and she repeated "The Turkey and the
Ant" and "The Fox at the Point of Death"
so playfully and well, that we very much

enjoyed the ant's snubbing the greedy old
bird, and the pretended repentance of sly
Reynard.

In the evening, with the crimson and gold
of the setting sun shining through the avenue
trees, Peep and I had a delightful walk back,
— Sir James and his wife and children accom-
panying us as far as the ivy-covered gates,
and bidding us good-by there with many
kind messages to Uncle and Aunty, and hopes
that we should find her headache quite passed
away. This was the case; and they were both
ready to listen to our account of our day's
pleasure.

It did us lasting good, too; for we began
learning round-singing and fable-repeating
with Aunt Pen, which made us pass many a
happy hour of an evening when Uncle came
home. Sometimes we had rounds, sometimes
songs, sometimes fables or short verse-pieces,
and sometimes Aunty would "tell us a story"
again. Time passed very fast, and we found
ourselves near the midsummer holidays, when
Tom was coming home.

We made a feast to receive him; Aunty and I ordering the dishes I knew he best liked for dinner, and decking the table with garlands and bunches of flowers, of which there were by this time plenty. Our garden, which had always been famous for being full of roses, supplied heaps and heaps of them, — white, blush, pale yellow, delicate pink, rich damask red, and clusters of noisettes and banksias. Ned Carter had done his very best, and had proved himself a capital gardener, contriving to have the bushes and standards and climbers in full bloom just the very week " Master Tom " was expected.

When he came, however, he did n't much notice the flowers; and even when I drew his attention to them, and told him how I had helped Aunt Pen to arrange them, he said, —

" What do I care about flowers? Flowers are well enough for women and girls to fuss over, but boys don't think much of them. What a row *you* make about 'em, Bab, you see! Yet what are they? Only a lot of roses, that are as common as cabbages. You should have seen the cape-jessamines and heliotropes and orchids at Wentworth Hall; they were something like, now!"

"Like what?" I said.

"Oh, well, like — like — anything. Like choice flowers. You know what I mean, Bab."

"But why should n't you like roses because they're common, — common as cabbages, as you say? Cabbages are very good things, I think, and so are cabbage-roses," said Aunt Pen, laughing.

Tom did n't even look towards her, and gave her no answer.

"Cabbages are one of my favorite vegetables," I said; "and cabbage-roses — roses of all sorts and kinds — are my favorite flowers."

"Ah, that's because you 're a little stay-at-home chit, Bab, who have scarcely seen any other flowers than roses," said Tom.

"Oh, yes; I 've seen camellias at Botterby House; and both Peep and I like our own roses a great deal better."

"'Birds of a feather flock together,' and

you and he are a couple of young geese, fool-
ish goslings. Oh, there's father at last," said
Tom, interrupting himself to look out of the
window, where he saw Uncle coming up the
garden path to the house.

I noticed that Tom's manner was changed
while his father was present. When Uncle
was at home, Tom was civilish and quietish,
though rather sulky and silent; but when
Uncle was out of the house, Tom was bluff
and rude to Peep and me, and very insolent
to Aunt Pen, — that is, he was insolent without saying a single word to her. He never
looked at her, never seemed to hear her
when she spoke, never addressed her or
answered her, never appeared to know that
she was in the room or even in the house.

One morning, as soon as Uncle was off to
town, Tom went up to his own room and
came down again with something in his hand,
which, after looking at for a moment, I could
n't make out.

"What's that, Tom?" I asked.

"A pistol. I'm going to practise my pistol-

shooting. I don't want to get out of practice.
I got to be a capital shot among the fellows at
school, and I shall lose my sure aim if I don't
keep it up."

" A pistol is a dangerous toy," said Aunt
Pen, quietly.

As usual, he took no notice of her having
spoken, and went on : " It's capital fun, when
you get to be a good shot. You can come
out and watch me, if you ain't afraid, Peep ?"

" I'm not afraid, Tom."

" Stand well at a distance, Peep," said Aunt
Pen ; adding, in her gentle but firm voice,
" pistols are dangerous toys."

But again Tom looked as if he had n't
heard her speak, and only said, —

" Come, Peep, if you care to come."

I felt fidgety about Peep's going out to
look on at the shooting, and I followed him
into the garden as he eagerly ran after Tom.
What with my feeling afraid about Peep, and
what with the startling bang of the noise the
pistol made whenever Tom let it off, I could
hardly help screaming every time he did so ;

but I managed to keep my scream pretty well in, though not quite.

"Girls are wretched cowards," said Tom. "What a piece of work they always make about guns and pistols, even if they're not loaded! And as to keeping from squeaking when fire-arms are let off, they can't for the life of them do it."

"I try not to scream; I try not to start, indeed, Tom; but I really cannot *quite* help doing both."

"I say so, — girls are a parcel of cowards, and we can't expect any better of them."

"Boys are cowards too, sometimes, and in some things," said Peep.

"Boys? What nonsense! Boys are always brave; that is, if they've anything in them at all. Why, I remember you yourself, Peep, when you were quite a little chap, and though it was against myself, you took my fancy by your plucky way of smashing my face with a shell when you thought I was vexing Bab."

"I'm not thinking of being cowardly in things like that. Every boy would be brave when he saw his sister being teased and could n't help herself. But what I am thinking about is being a coward in other things, — being afraid to behave as rudely to a person when somebody they 're obliged to behave well before is in the room as they do when he 's not."

"Is that meant for sauce, Master Peep?"

"It 's meant for truth," was the answer. "It 's true, and you know it, Tom, — that you behave very differently to Aunt Pen while Uncle 's away and when he 's at home; and I call that cowardly, — very mean."

"Mean?"

"Yes, mean, very mean; and not what any brave boy, any brave man, any true gentleman would do. He 'd scorn to be so mean, so cowardly."

"Upon my word, Master Peep, you 're turned parson, you preach so grandly. And to me, too, — your elder and your better."

"Elder, but not better," I said. "Peep 's good and true and brave to the backbone."

"A pretty joke, truly, — that I 'm come

home from school to be schooled and taken to task by two brats like you, and for a trumpery stitcher-for-her-bread like Pen Prim! A fine joke, upon my word!"

At that moment off went Tom's pistol, which he was holding carelessly in his pettish anger, and Peep, having in his eagerness of talk stepped a little forward from where he stood at first, received the charge in his cap, which fortunately he had put on when he went out. Tom was horribly frightened, and ran to Peep with, "Hullo, old fellow! I hope I have n't hit you."

"No, no; only my cap!" said Peep, good-humoredly.

"All right; but, by Jove, I thought the ball had gone through your head, my lad!"

"Pistols *are* dangerous toys," I said.

"Hold your nonsense, Miss Bab! Boys, if they want to be manly, should know how to use fire-arms."

"Boys, if they want to be manly, should practise pistol-firing when they 're not likely to shoot people through the head; and it is n't manly to insist on not hearing reason, or on being rude to those who talk reason, or on being mean and cowardly. *That* is n't manly."

" Bab, don't press him too hard," said Peep, as we turned to leave the garden.

" Girls always do press a fellow when they 've the right end of the stick," said Tom ; " but as they *are* girls, and can't fight, we let 'em have their say."

Nothing more was said. No mention was made of Peep's cap having had a bullet through it, for he was much too generous a little fellow either to tell tales or to bear malice for what was really an accident, though it might have been so serious for himself. Neither did Tom ever practise shooting again, nor did we ever even see his pistol any more. But he did not much mend his manners. It is true, he was no longer so actually insolent to Aunt Pen, but he grew more than ever sulky and silent and unsociable. At last, when Uncle noticed this one day, Tom said he felt bored.

" Bored, Tom, at home ? With us ?"

"Yes, with you all; I liked being at home for the holidays well enough when I had you to myself, father; but now there's such a lot of strangers in the house, I don't know it for the same."

"Strangers! Your cousins and my wife!"

"Yes, strangers; they're strange to me, and always will be. I don't feel at home with them; home isn't home now to me, and I don't care to come home."

"Not care to come home, Tom! Not care to be with me!"

"Well, as I can't have you without them, I don't care much even to be with you. You've got them and you don't want me. I'm getting tired, too, of school, and I want to go to sea. I should like it; I wish it; and I hope you'll let me go, father."

"I thought you liked your school and your schoolfellows so much, Tom."

"Ah, yes, I *did*; but I don't care even for school and the fellows there much now, since I've set my heart on going to sea. At sea, I shall be my own master, at least."

" Your own master at sea? Ah, Tom, you little know what going to sea is, if you say that."

" Let me try, father; let me try for myself; you went to sea, you know, when you were a lad, and I want to go. Don't say no, father. Let me go to sea."

" Well, my boy, you shall, if your heart is set upon it. At any rate, you shall try what the life is for a year, and then decide for yourself. If, after a long voyage, and going through all the hardships and discipline of a sailor's life, you still wish to make it your profession, you shall have your way; I won't thwart you."

" Thank you, father ! "

# CHAPTER XX.

THERE was to be a large garden-party for young people at Buckhurst Park, and we were all invited to go. Sue, who knew all the gossip and talk of the village told us that everybody was striving to get invitations, and that all the families round about were on thorns till the cards came which showed they were included. Uncle wished Aunty to order new dresses for herself and for me, in order to do proper honor to the occasion; but she said she meant to wear her delicate gray silk dress, that he had given her for one of her wedding dresses, and which she had scarcely worn more than a few times; while for me she intended to make a simple white muslin frock, which she thought the prettiest dress a little girl could have for a dancing-frock, and she had heard there was to be a ball after the entertainments in the garden.

" The Buckhursts themselves have set the excellent example of showing how little extravagance has to do with true taste, Uncle," she said; "and we cannot do better than follow so good an example. Besides, the gray silk and the white muslin are really the very most suitable things we could choose for this garden-party and dance. You 'll see how well Bab and I will look, and what credit we shall do you. But I think you will have to order a dress-suit for the boys, as their every-day clothes are a little rough-looking for such an occasion as this."

" Well, my Penn'orth, when you go out to-day you can tell Fitwell the tailor to step up here to-morrow morning and take Tom's and Peep's measure. Meantime, I'm off to town!"

Aunty let me help her in making up my muslin frock, by running the seams while she cut out the bodice and set it together. She put rows and rows of tucks round the skirt, as she said they were quite the prettiest and simplest trimming for a little girl's dress; and certainly it looked the freshest, daintiest frock possible, when it was finished.

Finding Tom and Peep in the garden that afternoon, I told them about Fitwell being ordered to come up next morning and take their measure.

"Not mine," said Tom; "I shall wear what I wore at Wentworth Hall. Thank her for nothing! As if I'd let Pen Prim meddle with my clothes! Thank ye, not I!"

"And yet it was she who got you to have that very dress-suit you had at Wentworth Hall," said Peep. "She asked Uncle to let you have an extra allowance when you wrote to him for more money for things you would want at Wentworth Hall."

"*She* asked him! Just like her meddling ways! I wish she'd let me alone!"

"Oh, Tom, how can you be so ungracious, so ungrateful?" I said.

"I don't want to be grateful to *her*. She's a meddling cat!"

"She always meddles — as you call it — for kindness and for good!"

"I don't want her kindness, or her good. I only wish her to leave me alone. I suppose she's going too, to this garden-party?"

"Of course."

"Well, one comfort of such parties is, they're so large, so full of company, and in such a great space, that one can keep clear of people one doesn't want to mix with."

When the day of the garden-party came, the carriage was sent for us from Buckhurst Park, and we had the pleasure of introducing Uncle to all the beauties of the place as we drove along; for he didn't go up to town for once, that he might enjoy this special holiday with us. Peep gave up his place on the coach-box to Tom, who said he liked to watch the horses.

Little Mabel came flying out to meet us as we stepped from the carriage. She looked quite a little fairy in her white frock, with blue ribbons on her shoulders like wings, and her hands full of flowers that she brought for

19

Aunty and me to wear in the front of our dresses. She had one herself among her bright curls, and she insisted on sticking one into my hair, — a rosebud exactly like the one she wore. She also put a little bunch of lilies-of-the-valley into my bodice and one into her own; as she said she wished us to be as alike as possible. Tom was very much struck with her prettiness, and whispered to me, as soon as she had flown off to welcome other guests, how extremely he admired her.

The garden-party was charming; the grass looked as if it were covered with blossoms as the ladies and children in their bright-colored dresses walked and ran about and played at various games, or stood still to listen to some beautiful part singing that was going on at one end of the lawn; while later on, at the other end, a band struck up, and the dancers began to think of choosing their partners.

"Bab," said Tom, "I should like you to introduce me to your pretty little friend Mabel, as I want very much to dance with her; but I suppose I ought to ask you first, as you're my oldest acquaintance here. Should you mind if I took her out before you?"

"I? Oh, not at all! I should be glad; for I'm engaged to William for the first dance."

"William? Who's he?"

"William Buckhurst,—that tall boy over there, with the curly brown hair. Haven't you been introduced to him yet?"

"I've been introduced to nobody. You've all been too busy with each other — you who are already such great friends — to mind about me. You never noticed or cared whether I was introduced or not."

"No, Tom, it wasn't that, indeed; it was because I never could get a sight of you, you kept so out of the way. Where were you?"

"Oh, I was over there among that clump of hawthorn-trees. I amused myself looking on, and watching the others. I didn't care to be among a parcel of strangers, that I didn't know one from another."

"If you kept apart, out of the way, how could I introduce you, Tom?"

" Well, introduce me now.   Introduce me to
your pretty little mite of a Mabel.   It 's a pity
she 's so very small, so very young ; but still
I should like her for a partner, for all that."

We made our way through the crowd of
eager, bright, gay girls and boys, all bent
upon their own particular partners either
already secured or being sought for, and at
last found ourselves near to Mabel Buckhurst,
who, with her cheeks rosy from running
about, and her eyes sparkling with delight at
the idea of dancing, certainly looked prettier
than ever.

" Mabel, dear (for she had long since told
me to call her " Mabel," as she called me
" Bab "), I 've brought you my cousin Tom
Bruff, who wishes to be presented to you,
that he may ask you to dance the first dance
with him."

" I can't ; I 've already promised your
brother Peep to dance it with him."

Tom bit his lip and looked furious.

" With   him, — with   that   little   chap ?
Why, he 's hardly more  than  a  baby ! "

"I'm hardly more than a baby myself," said she; "and if Peep's little, I'm littler. We shall make a capital couple, — an exact pair."

She dropped Tom a saucy little courtesy, and flew off to give her hand to Peep. I think I had never seen Tom look so black before, though I had often seen his face very dark and scowling. It looked black and blank too, as he stood frowning and staring on the ground.

"Stay; I see some one over there I know, Tom, and I'll introduce you to her if you like."

"Ay, do! But who is she? Which is she?"

"It's that young lady in the pink silk, over there talking to William. She's the rich Miss Botterby; she said she should be an heiress some day, and she's very good-natured and generous with her money, — that is, with her father's money; for he refuses her nothing, she told me so, and her mother is very indulgent to her too. They make a great deal of her, and she's thought very much of in her neighborhood."

"She's rather good-looking," said Tom. "Yes, Bab, you may introduce me to her."

We crossed to the spot where Miss Botterby stood smiling at William and talking very fast to him. She turned to me as soon as she saw me, with many assurances that she was *so* glad to meet me again.

"I've a crow to pick with you, though, now I come to think of it. How is it you've never been to Botterby House again, you naughty little creature you? But never mind, I won't begin by scolding you. I'm so pleased to see you again, any way, that I'll forgive you without more to-do."

I introduced Tom to her. He made his bow and asked her hand for the first dance.

"Oh, you're very good, I'm sure; but I rather think, — I believe — I — "

She simpered, looked down at her fan, and then gave a side glance at William, who waited quietly and silently till she finished her speech.

"I half thought I was already engaged; but I remember now, I'm not. I shall be very happy to give you the first dance."

She courtesied to Tom, who led her off to join the dancers, now beginning to form for the first set, which was to be a country-dance.

"We shall be the top couple, I suppose," I heard her say, as they moved away.

"I fancy not," was the answer; "Miss Mabel Buckhurst, who is the young lady of the house, may perhaps lead off."

"Hardly, I should think," said Miss Botterby, tossing her head; "that would be strange etiquette indeed. The daughter of the house is the last person who should take the lead. Get me a place as near the top as you can, please."

To my great surprise I found that *I*, of all little people in the world, had to lead off; for it was settled that William (as son of the house) and his partner should be top couple. I felt a little — a very little — afraid, on finding myself obliged to begin the dance, and hoped I might not be too shy or too awkward to do William credit, who was a very graceful dancer; but Aunty had taught Peep and me so well our first steps and positions, and had so often made Uncle and us two stand up with her for a dancing-lesson of an evening, that we both acquitted ourselves very fairly; and she told us so when we reached home after our pleasant day of the garden-party and dance at Buckhurst Park.

It was long a subject of talk and bright recollection afterwards; but next morning when Tom, Peep, and I were in the garden together Tom said suddenly, —

"Bab, promise me that while I'm away you won't dance any more with William Buckhurst. There's something about that fellow I detest; and I don't like to think of your dancing with him."

"Why?"

"Oh, I don't exactly know; but I find him an insufferable puppy, and I don't care to have you his partner any more."

"But suppose I care; suppose I like him, —

which I do very much. He's manly and
gentlemanly and gentle, and I like him; he's
a very good dancer too, and it's pleasant to
have him for a partner."

" But if I don't like him?"

"I can't help that; I'm sorry you don't,
and I think it's a pity — for yourself, Tom.
But I can't help it if you don't like him; and
I don't see why your not liking him should
prevent my liking him."

" Yes, it ought; I'm your cousin; you've
known me much before you knew him, and
my likings and dislikings ought to have some
weight with you, Bab."

"I don't see at all why they should, especially when they're unreasonable. You say
you don't know *why* you dislike William, you
can't give a reason for your not liking him;
therefore I can't see why I should give up my
liking to please a whim of yours."

" If you cared for me, — if you cared for
my opinion, — you would do as I ask you."

" Not if you ask me to do what is unreasonable."

"Reasonable or unreasonable, you ought to oblige me if you can."

"But I can't oblige you in this; do not ask it, Tom."

"Then you won't give up dancing with this fellow? It's a small thing to ask; will you grant it me, Bab?"

"No, Tom!"

He ground his teeth hard, looked at me fiercely, and then said, —

"I could wring your neck at this moment, Bab!"

There was a pause, a silence, and then he continued, —

"I suppose you won't even shake hands with me when I go to sea?"

"Yes, I will! Why not? I'll even now shake hands with you, — at once, Tom."

I held out my hand to him; he took it in his, and gripped it rather roughly, then let it drop.

"And will you say good-by to me when I go?"

"Of course, Tom."

" Say it now, Bab."

" Good-by, Tom."

He snatched my hand again, looking hard at me, then flung it from him, turned on his heel, and tried to whistle as he went away.

" I can't bear Tom, I never could!" exclaimed Peep. " Wring your neck, indeed! I like that! "

" No, you don't, Peep."

" I mean, catch me standing by and letting him do it! "

" I think he tries to be kind, Peep; but somehow he seems as if he could n't be."

" It's no use, Bab; I can't bear him, and I never could! "

Next morning when we all came down to breakfast there was no Tom. Before it was light he had left home for London to join his ship, on board of which Uncle had procured him a berth as cabin-boy, which was his own wish. It seems he had taken leave of his father overnight, and said he did n't want good-byes with any one else. Uncle looked rather disturbed and thoughtful that day, and for some days after; but Aunt Pen did all she could to cheer him, and Peep and I did our best to amuse him, and prevent him from feeling sad.

At the end of a fortnight came a letter from Tom to his father, written in the highest spirits, saying his ship was on the point of sailing, that he liked his captain and his ship-mates, and was now "as jolly and free as could be."

Our little home party fell into its old pleas-ant ways, and as we sat at breakfast one bright summer morning looking at Aunt Pen, who had just said something in her gentle way that made us all break into a hearty laugh, I thought, "I really do believe there are not happier people in the whole wide world than

AUNTY, UNCLE, PEEP, AND I!"

University Press: John Wilson & Son, Cambridge.

# SUSAN COOLIDGE'S POPULAR BOOKS.

THE CLIFFS.

## A LITTLE COUNTRY GIRL.
**With Illustrations.**

One volume. Square 16mo. Cloth, black and gold. Price $1.50.

ROBERTS BROTHERS, PUBLISHERS, *Boston.*

# JOLLY GOOD TIMES;

OR,

## CHILD LIFE ON A FARM.

By P. THORNE.    Price $1.25.

ROBERTS BROTHERS, Publishers,

SIX TO SIXTEEN.   A Story for Girls.   By Mrs.
Ewing.   Price $1.00.

ROBERTS BROTHERS, Publishers,

*Boston.*

# CASTLE BLAIR:

## *A STORY OF YOUTHFUL DAYS.*

### By FLORA L. SHAW.

16mo. Cloth. Price $1.00.

" There is quite a lovely little book just come out about children, — ' Castle Blair ! ' . . . The book is good, and lovely, and true, having the best description of a noble child in it (Winnie) that I ever read ; and nearly the best description of the next best thing, — a noble dog," says John Ruskin, the distinguished art critic.

" 'Castle Blair,' a story of youthful days, by Flora L. Shaw, is an Irish story. A charming young girl — half French, half English — comes from France, at the age of eighteen, to live with her bachelor uncle at Castle Blair, which is in possession of five children of an absent brother of this uncle. The children are in a somewhat wild and undisciplined condition, but they are as interesting children as can be imagined, and some of them winning to an extraordinary degree. They are natural children, in manner and in talk ; but the book differs from some American books about children, in that it is pervaded by an air of refinement and good-breeding. The story is altogether delightful, quite worthy, from an American point of view, of all Mr. Ruskin says of it ; and if circulation were determined by merit, it would speedily outstrip a good many now popular children's books which have a vein of commonness, if not of vulgarity." — *Hartford Courant.*

" It is not too much to say that nothing more interesting or more wholesome is offered this year for older boys and girls. It is a charming story, in which the author has delineated character as carefully, and with as keen an artistic sense, as if she had been writing a novel. Her book is a novel, indeed, with children and the lives of children, instead of men and women and their lives, for its theme." — *New York Evening Post.*

*Our publications are to be had of all Booksellers. When not to be found, send directly to*

### ROBERTS BROTHERS, Publishers,
#### BOSTON

www.ingramcontent.com/pod-product-compliance
Lightning Source LLC
Chambersburg PA
CBHW060558030726
47498CB00005B/1440